OPPOSITES ATTRACT

Jeb Marlow was not happy to trust his life to the young pilot who was to fly him through a New Zealand mountain range in poor weather. What was more, the pilot was a girl. Though they were attracted, Jacquetta soon realised they lived in different worlds; he had a champagne lifestyle, dashing around the world, and she helped run an isolated fruit farm in New Zealand. Could they ever have any sort of relationship or would their differences always come between them?

CHRISSIE LOVEDAY

OPPOSITES ATTRACT

Complete and Unabridged

LINFORD
Leicester

First published in Great Britain in 2005

First Linford Edition
published 2005

British Library CIP Data

Loveday, Chrissie
   Opposites attract.—Large print ed.—
Linford romance library
   1. Women air pilots—Fiction 2. New
Zealand—Fiction 3. Love stories
   4. Large type books
   I. Title
   823.9'14 [F]

   ISBN 1–84395–934–8

Published by
F. A. Thorpe (Publishing)
Anstey, Leicestershire

Set by Words & Graphics Ltd.
Anstey, Leicestershire
Printed and bound in Great Britain by
T. J. International Ltd., Padstow, Cornwall

This book is printed on acid-free paper

1

The man pulled his collar up to protect himself from unrelenting drizzle. He glanced at his watch and stamped his feet impatiently. Evidently, he was not used to waiting.

'I should never have let that taxi go,' he muttered angrily. 'He must have brought me to the wrong place.'

The great open field and a couple of sheds could hardly be described as an airport. He cursed his father for sending him to New Zealand's South Island. What did he hope to gain by opening another hotel? The profits here would be nothing compared with the huge city-centre hotels that had made the family fortune. But his father was the boss. As the only son, it was Jeb Marlow's job to do all the leg work.

His flight should be leaving at nine-thirty and so far, he couldn't even see a plane, let alone a check-in desk. He noticed a cupboard with **Telephone** written on it. He dialled the number given for the airport manager.

Eventually, a sleepy voice answered.

''Mornin', how can I help?'

'I am expecting a flight out in four minutes and there's nobody here. What's going on?'

'Sorry, mate. I don't think we had any flights scheduled for today. Hang on there awhiles and I'll see what I can find out. Don't go away.'

'Fat chance, unless I walk several miles.'

He stamped his feet for a few seemingly endless seconds.

'Hi. You still there?'

'Like I said, there's nowhere else to go. Well?'

'There's someone on their way. Pilot should be with you any time. Jack's flying you out today. OK, mate? See you.'

Jeb Marlow stared at the handset in disbelief. That was really the airport manager? And his father seriously wanted to open a hotel here? He glanced around as he heard a motor-bike approaching. Two figures, clad entirely in black leathers, were on the back.

'That's all I need,' he murmured. 'Mugged by a couple of bikers.'

They stopped in front of him. The shorter one dismounted and Jeb clutched his briefcase tighter, ready in case of attack, even though the opponent was no match for his six-foot-two frame. The guy could only be about five-eight at most.

The leather-clad figure hauled off a travel bag and pulled off the helmet, shouting thanks. The driver acknow-ledged the words with a wave and roared away. Jeb's jaw dropped as the girl came towards him. She had long light-brown hair, dragged back into a pony-tail, and looked all of fifteen. She extended a hand to him.

'Good morning, sir. I'm your pilot for today.'

Her deep brown eyes danced with mischief as she acknowledged his surprise.

'So what happened to Jack?'

'That's me. Jacquetta Goodman. Everyone, just about, calls me Jacq. You must be Mr Marsh.'

'Er, yes, that's right.'

He always travelled as Marsh, as he got more honest answers than when he admitted his real name. Everyone knew of Marlow Hotels.

'Look,' he went on, 'I guess there's been some sort of error. I booked a flight to Queenstown this morning. I have an important meeting at eleven-thirty and I was assured that there was a suitable flight.'

'The regular pilot has gone down with some bug and as I was going back to Queenstown, this seemed like an obvious solution. They'll pick up the plane from there, later.'

She gave him a dazzling smile to which at any other time he might have responded. Even if she was only a kid,

4

she was certainly a looker.

'Just assuming you were either old enough or capable of flying a plane, where is there anything to fly?'

'Cessna, round the back of the hangar. It's almost new, delivered it myself, a couple of days back. Oh, and by the way, I am both old enough and a fully-qualified pilot. We start flying young in this country!'

'A Cessna? You propose to fly me in that tiny crate?'

He shook his head in disbelief.

'I'll get it untied,' the girl said. 'I'll taxi round for you and your luggage.'

She walked off briskly, and disappeared behind the corrugated shed. Reluctantly, he picked up his travel bag and briefcase and followed her. He could at least reassure himself that the plane was airworthy.

'OK,' she announced, 'she's all ready. You want to climb in here or round the front of the building?'

'Next to the check-in, I suppose,' he muttered sarcastically.

'Oh, yes. You got your ticket?' she asked.

He produced the soft leather travel document wallet supplied by the travel agent and peeled off the appropriate ticket. She rolled it up and stuffed it in her pocket, scarcely glancing at it.

'OK,' she said with a grin, 'bit too noisy to talk much once we get going. We shall be following the river route. Only problem is, it's rather misty and the forecast's bad. If we can't get through, I'll have to try the other side of the mountain.'

Shaking his head in disbelief, he clambered up into the tiny plane.

'Strap yourself in,' she ordered and with an irritated glare, he buckled the seat-belt. He should have kept the hire car and driven. Was he really letting himself fly through a mountain range with a kid who looked scarcely old enough to drive, let alone fly a plane?

'Used to work down here, doing scenic flights over Milford Sound. Beautiful on a good day,' she shouted.

'You been to see it?'

He shook his head.

'No time. Business trip.'

The noise was deafening as they taxied along the runway and with a judder and much rattling, the little plane lifted off the ground. However many flights he had taken, Jeb knew this was something completely different.

The scenery below was undoubtedly spectacular, even covered in misty drizzle. The mountains were almost hidden and he hoped the girl had enough experience of the area to guide them through. He watched her every move closely as she scanned the ground beneath them.

'Have to come down a bit,' she shouted. 'Don't like the way the mist is closing in. It could be even worse farther on.'

They dropped down a few hundred feet until they were almost skimming the treetops. Sheep scattered over the fields as the little plane flew over them.

His heart was pounding with fear. She was muttering into the lip microphone and he strained to catch what she was saying. Each second, he felt panic growing.

'Everything all right?' he called out anxiously.

She moved the headset to one side and shouted back.

'I don't like this weather. I'm going to try the other valley. I don't want to fly into any mountains.'

The prospect of flying blind through a mountain range did not appeal to him one bit. The most sophisticated equipment on board seemed to be the radio. He gripped his seat tightly. She turned the little plane and soon they were backtracking.

Just before they reached the airfield, she veered off to the right, to follow another valley. The lakes gleamed below them, glassy surfaces barely showing a ripple from this height.

The trees looked like their own version of the sea, regular green waves of pine forest, stretching endlessly. Everywhere looked lush and very green, not surprising with this rainfall.

The engine droned on and the rain started to come down more heavily. Jacq spoke into her lip-mike again and then, shoving it aside, called out to Jeb.

'Look, I'm sorry, but I have to turn back. I just daren't risk it. Queenstown says it's clear there but really bad to the south. I'm sorry.'

Wretched girl could hardly be blamed for the weather but if the pilot had had a bit more experience, a well-qualified bloke, they might have made it. As for this silly little plane, how could they pretend it was a scheduled flight?

'So how do I get from here to Queenstown?' he demanded.

'I've radioed the service bus. He's diverting to the airfield to pick us up,' the girl shouted back.

He shook his head. A service bus! This girl shouldn't be trying to do man's work. He'd complain, if he ever reached Queenstown.

The rain closed in. A flicker of alarm crossed the girl's face and Jeb felt his insides clenching. She scanned the dials, biting her lip. Jeb desperately tried to remember the safety guidance he usually ignored. What was it, head down and brace against the seat? Suddenly, the engine changed tone and they dropped into solid grey mist. He instinctively put his arms up to cover his face, awaiting impact, but they touched down with only the slightest judder. He'd known worse landings in a Jumbo! Grudgingly, he admitted her skill as the little plane taxied towards the hangar.

It was ten-thirty, barely an hour since they left on this fool's errand. They should have been in Queenstown by now.

'I'm really sorry, but there was no other choice,' she said.

'Pity you didn't realise before we started. You haven't heard the end of this, you know. I have totally wasted a valuable hour of my time, and I still have to get to Queenstown.'

He paused to draw breath and noticed the distress in her deep brown eyes.

'OK, I suppose it wasn't your fault,' he admitted. 'It doesn't help me and my meeting. Is it always this bad down here?'

'Used to be when I worked the area. I've been back home for a couple of years, on North Island.'

'Please, can you call a taxi for me? Radio them or something? And I have to speak to my colleagues. My mobile doesn't work here.'

'There's a phone by the service area back there,' she snapped. 'The bus is diverting to collect us. There are no taxis, anyhow. The bus should be here soon and even allowing for stops, it will get you there in about two and a half hours. Now, if you would kindly leave the aircraft, I'll bring your luggage around.'

Jeb was not used to taking orders.

11

Who did she think she was dealing with? Angrily, he unfastened his seat-belt and reached into the back for his bags. He also picked up her holdall and leaped down to the ground.

'I can manage my own bag, thanks,' she called.

She was not looking forward to a long bus ride home with this bad-tempered individual. The weather was hardly her fault, neither was the bug that had hit the local pilot. She had been doing them a favour.

'When's this cursed bus due?' he asked at the very moment the service bus rattled into the driveway.

The driver got out and came over to chat to Jacq. Jeb picked up his bags and walked towards the doorway.

'Hang on a minute. I'll put the bags in the back. Not much room in there,' the driver called.

'I'll keep them with me. I might do a bit of work during the drive.'

'You won't mate, not the way this old crate bumps along,' the driver said and laughed, seizing the bag and stowing it in a compartment at the rear. 'Got a full load. Guess you'll both have to ride up-front with me, in the noisy seats.'

With a venomous look at everyone, Jeb climbed on board. This day was turning into a nightmare. In half an hour's time, he should have been sitting chairing a meeting, sipping good coffee, followed by a beautifully-prepared luncheon. He had been looking forward to the excellent ice-cold Sauvignon Blanc they'd recently contracted from the Marlborough vineyards. Now he would be lucky to make it for coffee after lunch, if this old heap made it back to Queenstown at all.

Jacq sat beside him, chatting and smiling to the driver. She relaxed once the journey started and took a surreptitious look at her passenger. She was surprised at the effect he had on her. Despite his rude, overbearing behaviour, he was the best-looking man she had seen in ages. She blushed at her own thoughts as she pulled the clip holding back her hair.

Jeb glanced at her. Her hair flowed down her back, long and silky with curling tendrils that framed a lovely face. Free of the ugly head-set, he could see that she was a beautiful young woman. Given some decent clothes, make-up and a manicure, she would easily outdo any fashionable women who usually hung on to his arm. Her clear complexion and perfect skin gave her a head start. He suddenly felt the urge to apologise for his rudeness.

'Look,' he said, 'I'm sorry if I seemed rude. I'm under a lot of pressure. It's an important meeting I really can't afford to miss. But, maybe I was a bit hard on you.'

'Sorry?' she shouted back. 'Couldn't hear.'

'Nothing. Doesn't matter,' he yelled.

He turned the other way and looked through the side window. He could see her reflection. She turned to look at him again and he was aware of her scrutiny. He gave the ghost of a smile at her and settled back in his seat. He closed his eyes, as if to discourage further conversation. He was almost dozing when the bus screeched to a halt. Several of the passengers were leaving. They stood chatting to the driver as the minutes ticked by.

'What time are we likely to get in?' he asked Jacq.

'Should be there about one, I guess.'

'Depending on how many friends and relations our friend has to stop and chat to, I suppose,' he muttered.

'All OK?' the driver asked.

This had to be one of the most extraordinary journeys of this life, Jeb thought. He had flown all over the world. He always used first-class travel and was not used to this. He felt starving. As if reading his mind, Jacq leaned towards him.

'Piece of chocolate?' she offered.

'Thanks,' he said gratefully.

He smiled his gratitude, warmed by the tiny gesture of communication with this extraordinary woman. Only the briefest conversation was possible. Pity, he thought. Jacq might have proved to be an interesting lady. Perhaps they might see something of each other if she was staying in town for a few days. There was certainly no-one else in the town who was likely to entertain him.

Once today's meetings were through, he had some free time. He could invite her to dinner, as compensation for his bad temper.

As they left the higher mountain passes, the cloud began to lift. It was breathtakingly beautiful, the mountains dropping steeply to the far shoreline of the lake, as they came towards Queenstown. The driver pulled up in the bus station. He got out and hauled luggage from the back. Jeb collected his bags.

'Where you staying, mister?' the driver asked.

'The Marlow.'

'I'll drop you there if you like. No worries,' he offered. 'How about you, Jacq? You got somewhere to stay?'

'Not yet. I'll have to find somewhere.

Not the Marlow,' she added ruefully. 'I'm not on expenses so I'll be looking for something a bit less grand.'

'Why not try it? Perhaps they'll have something at special rates,' Jeb suggested.

He still felt slightly guilty about venting his temper on the girl. He'd already missed the meeting, so a few more minutes hardly mattered. He'd speak to the receptionist at the hotel and make certain she was quoted something she could afford. He would definitely invite her for dinner. He hated dining alone.

'I don't know,' she said doubtfully. 'The Marlow is much too expensive, whatever discount they may offer.'

Jeb shrugged.

'Suit yourself. Why not walk with me anyhow? There may be somewhere else.'

Jacq nodded and picked up her travel bag. She hadn't got much in the way of clothing with her, just the basics for a few days' break in the holiday centre.

They strode towards the lakeside hotel, Jacq easily matching his pace, despite his long legs.

He was extremely good-looking, she had to admit. Early thirties, she estimated, dark hair, slightly curly and obviously very well cut. His dark brown eyes gave him an honest look, a clean-cut, boy-next-door impression, but she sensed that was just a front. She had first-hand experience of his temper when things went wrong.

Once they reached the hotel, he swept inside, ushering her in front of him. The gleaming marble floors led towards the magnificent reception desk.

'Hang on a minute,' he ordered Jacq. 'I'll have a word with the clerk. See if they can do a special deal.'

She hesitated. It was all too grand for her. She just needed a bed somewhere, nothing as expensive as this must be. She watched Jeb in action with a slight smile pushing at the corners of her mouth. He had a commanding air about him. People automatically knew that he would not tolerate anything but the very best. She smiled to herself, seeing him in natural surroundings. He must have really loved that little god-forsaken airstrip! The receptionist was nodding and smiling almost deferentially, she thought. He turned and beckoned her over.

'They've got some little single room tucked away. It's usually used when parents need a second room for a child so it's not very grand. You can have it for a couple of nights if you're interested. Only a few dollars,' he said.

'Well, If you're sure it's really cheap.'

The receptionist gave her a price and she stared. It was less than she had been expecting to pay anywhere in Queenstown.

'Done,' she replied happily, taking the registration card and filling it in, before anyone could change their minds!

Whatever the room was like, she wasn't about to refuse this good an offer. She took the key and picked up her holdall.

'Thanks very much. I don't know what you said to her, but even a broom cupboard would be good for that price!'

Her eyes were dancing as if filled with her own pleasure of life. Jeb smiled, liking what he saw. She seemed so genuine. There were none of the pretences or posturing he saw in so many women. They bored him, these ladies who seemed to think they had to impress him with their worldliness.

'How about joining me for dinner tonight? Nothing worse than eating alone. You'd be doing me a real favour.'

He put on his most charming smile, hoping to persuade her.

'Besides,' he continued, 'I owe you, for my bad temper this morning.'

'You were a monster, but I haven't got any decent clothes, not for a place like this. I came with minimum luggage. There isn't much room in a Cessna, especially when it's full of fuel.'

'We can eat somewhere else, if it

20

bothers you. Just wear your smile, forget the clothes,' he suggested with a devilish grin.

'OK, thanks!' She laughed. 'I would really prefer somewhere less posh. I'd hate to be drummed out of the dining-room for wearing trousers!'

'Meet me down here at six-thirty. We'll decide what to do then.'

He turned around and walked to the elevator. She watched him, frowned slightly and went to find her broom cupboard.

2

As broom cupboards went, this one had an air of luxury. The room was not exactly large but it had a shower en-suite. It may not have a lake view but the garden outside was colourful and bright. Jacq could hardly believe her luck. It was a ridiculously cheap tariff, even for a child's room.

She took a quick shower and pulled on a clean T-shirt. The weather was pleasantly warm after the damp start. She deposited her key and went to explore the town.

There seemed to be a holiday atmosphere everywhere. The shops were full of adverts for trips, flights, boat rides and dozens of other touristy things. She went into a fast-food restaurant and ordered a piece of fried chicken. It was almost two-thirty and she hadn't eaten since breakfast.

After her snack, she wandered around the shops, making plans for her short stay. She would try some of the trips she had never had the time to do when she had worked in the area, do all the things her customers had raved about. She glanced up at the sky gondolas, making non-stop journeys to the summit of Bob's Peak. Perhaps tomorrow? Maybe she could look at the shops to find a couple of small presents for Jamylla, her twin sister, and Dad.

Life had been tough for them all over the past years, but things were improving gradually. The death of her mother nine years ago had dealt them the first huge blow and Dad had never entirely come to terms with it. Their farm seemed to have lost its mainstay and several times, he had almost given up. But the kiwi fruit orchards, together with the market-garden style vegetable production and the riding stables, gave the family a reasonable income and certainly plenty of work to do. It seemed a million miles away from this place.

She felt a pang of homesickness. She longed for the peace and tranquillity of their farm. It was odd, as most of the time she and Jamie complained bitterly about their solitary lives. She glanced at her watch. She would have time for a short rest before she met up with her ex-passenger. She felt a slight frisson of anticipation. It was good to have someone new to share time with, especially a good-looking man like Jeb Marsh, even if he was bad-tempered!

She wondered what his so important work entailed. He was obviously high-powered and judging by his accent, he was visiting the country from the UK. She wondered what he had been doing in the South.

As she waited for him back at the hotel, Jacq watched the other guests. She certainly needn't worry about being smart enough for the hotel. People wore everything from long, dressy evening skirts to brightly-coloured shorts. Her mother would have been horrified at the thought of someone eating dinner wearing shorts, but then, her mother had always been a little old-fashioned about such things. This was a holiday town and everyone was much more relaxed than in the staid, conventional confines of Wharenui.

He was late, almost ten minutes late. Perhaps he had thought better of his offer and something or someone more suitable had turned up. She would give him five more minutes and then leave a message at reception and go out to find her own dinner.

At six-forty-five, Jacq walked over to the receptionist. The immaculately-groomed woman smiled, displaying even, white teeth. The long, red-lacquered nails tapped gently, as she waited to hear Jacq's request.

'May I leave a message for Jeb Marsh, please?' she asked. 'Tell him I waited till quarter to and assumed he was still busy.'

'Certainly, ma'am. Shall I phone to see if Mr Jeb is still in his suite?'

His suite? Wow! It must cost a fortune to have a suite here. Still, if he was on expenses, it probably meant nothing, and what was with the Mr Jeb routine? The long red nails clicked as she dialled a number.

'Sorry. He doesn't seem to be there. I'll pass on your message when he comes down.'

'And what message is that?' the voice behind her asked.

She swung round to see Jeb. He was dressed in beautifully-tailored light grey trousers and a blue open-neck shirt. It had the unmistakable sheen of pure silk and immediately, Jacq felt scruffy in her cotton shirt and twice-worn trousers.

'I thought you'd been held up. I was just going to find somewhere to eat for myself,' she said.

She couldn't understand why her heart was beating in this ridiculous way. He may be good-looking and obviously well-off, but he was just a bloke after all, wasn't he?

He smiled, the dark eyes crinkling at the corners.

'I seem to remember you kept me waiting for a good quarter of an hour this morning,' he said. 'Surely I deserve the same courtesy. I thought we'd go up to the top of the mountain on the gondola. There's a restaurant up there. Don't know what the food's like but the view should more than compensate.'

'Sounds great,' she agreed. 'I was planning to go up tomorrow but it would be nice to see the lights.'

It was a steep climb to the gondola station and they were both out of breath as they arrived.

'Two days sitting in an aircraft and I'm right out of condition,' Jacq said laughingly.

'I'm missing my work-outs,' Jeb admitted.

'Did you sort out your problems with the meeting?' she asked. 'You were supposed to be working today.'

'They had a preliminary, in my absence, and we've re-scheduled for breakfast tomorrow morning. I shouldn't have any problems.'

The winch droned on as they climbed higher and higher. They had the cabin to themselves and were able to look all round as they rose above the town. Jeb stared out the windows, torn between wanting to see the view and wanting to gaze into his companion's eyes. She had twisted her long hair into a loose top-knot, showing her slender neck to advantage. Even the baggy trousers could not hide her slim waist and perfect figure. She was certainly a beauty. The lack of sophisticated gloss gave her added charm and he knew he was going to enjoy her company.

Jacq was also studying her companion. She liked what she saw. The lean body had an easy grace. Whatever his job, he managed to keep himself in trim, probably by working out at some exclusive gym.

'So, tell me all about yourself,' he

invited, once they were seated in the restaurant.

'Pretty boring, really. I come from a place out in the sticks, well, halfway up a mountain, I suppose, up in North Island. It's called Wharenui, around fifty kilometres north of Rotorua,' she said, naming the one place everyone seemed to have heard of.

'Oh, right. Yes, I know Rotorua well. We have a hotel . . . I mean the people I work for have a hotel there.'

'What do you do?' she asked curiously.

'Sort of accountant, I suppose. Bit of a trouble shooter.'

'So how come you are travelling around, if you are an accountant? I thought they stayed in offices pressing keys on a computer all day long.'

'Shall we order? Goodness knows what the food is like, but I guess we're about to find out.'

His deft changing of the subject did not go unnoticed.

They had a bottle of New Zealand

red wine to accompany the almost inevitable roast lamb. The food was simple but well cooked and very substantial. Jeb leaned back in his chair and wiped his mouth with his napkin when he had finished.

'Not bad,' he said. 'I was certainly ready for that. I seem to have missed out on proper meals today and one thing guaranteed to make me bad-tempered is to miss a meal. Did I say sorry about my bad temper this morning?'

Jacq laughed.

'Only about ten times.'

She had enjoyed the evening. Though he had avoided telling her about himself, she had regaled him with tales of her own life. She told him about the farm and the kiwi orchards. She even described her favourite horse, Jasmin, who would let no-one else ride her. She told him how she and her sister had built up this side of the business, while Dad worked to develop the fruit growing and vegetable production. At busy times, they all had to pitch in and help.

'So where does the flying fit in?' he asked, leaning back in his seat.

'I just love it. All my life I wanted to fly and Dad gave me lessons for my birthday, as soon as I was old enough. I worked all over the country for a year or two, once I'd qualified. Loved the life. Never quite managed to buy my own plane. I almost bought a half-share in one. It didn't work out.'

'What happened?' Jeb asked.

'Someone I knew, well, still do really. He wanted us to get engaged, married, the whole bit. I was much too young to want to settle down like that. Heavens, I was only just over twenty years old. Hal was older, and felt the need to settle. I think the half-share in a plane was a sort of a bribe. It was through him I got to fly the Cessna down here. He wanted it delivering and thought I'd like the job, keep up my flying hours. He even gave some names of people to try for a ride back, though I did wonder whether to drive up and take the ferry back across to North Island. See a bit of countryside at ground level.'

'Suppose you know a lot of these flying types?' Jeb suggested.

'Almost like one big club, I guess. You come across them all over. It's quite a big country really, but with such a small population, you tend to meet up with folks more often than you'd think.'

'And is this Hal still serious about you?' he asked, suddenly realising he felt stupidly jealous at the thought of anyone being close to her.

Damn it, what was wrong with him? He'd only just met the girl and here he was behaving as if he'd bought shares in her. He'd probably never see her again after tonight.

'He'd like to be. He keeps saying my sister is practically settled, so surely I should be thinking about it.'

'Older or younger?' he asked. 'Your sister.'

'Older,' she said, a mischievous smile on her face.

It was the truth, but she failed to add

that Jamie was only five minutes older! She enjoyed teasing people, not telling them she had an identical twin. It was the typical childhood game, letting people mistake one for the other, especially if they didn't know there were two of them. She wondered why she had said nothing this time. She was never likely to see this man again, let alone have him meet her sister.

'And are you getting closer to wanting to settle down? You must be well over twenty by now, even if you do only look about fifteen in your flying gear.'

'You ask a lot of questions,' she said suddenly. 'How about telling me about you?'

'Accountants are notoriously boring,' he replied enigmatically. 'I'm the only son of a bossy father who seems to think I have nothing better to do with my time than rush around the world doing his bidding.'

'Hardly sounds boring, compared to my life.' Jacq smiled. 'The highlight of our social whirl is the Pickers' and Packers' Ball, once a year.'

'I like you,' he said suddenly. 'For once my father did me a favour, sending me to the back of beyond. Look, what are you doing for the next couple of days? I don't have anything pressing for a while. Perhaps we could do a few of the tourist things together. What do you say?'

'OK. Why not? I had planned to take in a few of the sights, except for bungee jumping. I'll try most things but I draw the line at that!'

'Shame on you.' He laughed. 'The one thing I wanted to do and she turns me down.'

'I'm not stopping you. I'll even come and watch, take photos if you like. But no way do I attach myself to a bit of elastic and leap off a bridge.'

'Don't think you'd catch me up there,' he replied. 'Jet boats are my limit for scary things to do.'

'Yes, I fancied that, too, and it'll be more fun with a friend.'

'Is that what we are? Friends?' Jeb asked softly.

'I guess,' she replied slowly, 'if that's what you want. Do you have to attach a label to everything?'

He leaned across the table and touched her fingers lightly.

'I think I'd like us to become very good friends, but if we don't either pay up or order something else, we are in danger of getting thrown out of this place. Besides, I don't fancy walking down this mountain, not in the dark.'

Jacq started. She had been drifting away into a strange sort of daydream. For one brief, mad second, she had seen herself taking Jeb home with her, introducing him to her father. Ridiculous nonsense! By the time she returned home in a few days, he would be far away, back in England, with never a thought of her in his mind.

'Yes, you're right. Everyone else has gone.'

Outside, there was a walkway round

the restaurant. There were lights glowing for miles in the clear night. Against the starlit sky, the black shapes of mountains could be seen.

'They say there's wonderful skiing up there in the winter. The mountains are called the Remarkables,' Jacq whispered dreamily.

'Yes, I know,' he replied. 'I visited a couple of years back. Came over on business and someone offered to take me.'

This guy was 'way out of her league, she thought. Anyone who flew around the world like he did was hardly going to be interested in someone from the sticks.

'So, jet boats in the morning? Come on. Let's go down.'

He took her hand and they walked together to the station. They were almost the only people left and again had the little car to themselves. Jacq felt almost shy with him, despite the shared evening. He remained strangely reticent to talk about himself and she realised she had discovered nothing about Mr Jeb Marsh.

They strolled back to the hotel, companionably, hand in hand. Before they reached the hotel grounds, he stopped and pulled her into his arms. She felt a sense of expectancy. Something inevitable was about to happen and suddenly, she felt as if she had known this man for years. His strong arms enfolded her slender body and drew her to him. As if in a dream, she floated there, waiting for his mouth to touch her own. She could feel his heart beating as his body pressed against her. Although they had only met that morning, it felt as though they had been destined specifically for this moment. She shivered, not just at the cold air.

'Let's go inside,' he murmured.

Surprisingly, this girl was something very special, he just knew it. He had never felt such a closeness, not this early in any of his previous friendships. He walked her in, a proprietorial arm round her slim waist. The receptionist looked up and gave them a knowing smile.

'Good evening, Mr Jeb, madam. Had a pleasant evening?'

'Any messages?' Jeb asked automatically.

'Your father called. He wants you to phone him back as soon as possible.'

Jeb glanced at his watch.

'He'll probably be at lunch, now. I'll do it later.'

'He said he'd wait. I did say you were out with a . . . with a friend. He said he'd be in his office anyhow.'

'Blast,' Jeb snapped. 'Thanks, Melissa. I'd better give him a call.'

'Can I have my key please?' Jacq asked.

'Oh, yes, certainly. Sorry. I assumed that . . . yes, sorry.'

She covered her confusion and turned to the row of keys hanging behind her, selecting Jacq's and handing it to her.

'Thank you. Good-night, Jeb, and

thanks for dinner,' Jacq said.

'Come and have a nightcap. My call won't take long. I have a bottle of champagne on ice, waiting just for you.'

She hesitated. Every part of her wanted to continue what they had started outside but she knew it would be playing with fire. It was obvious to the most innocent mind that the immaculate Melissa had expected her to accompany him to his suite. She must have sensed that Jacq was not quite his usual type, much too scruffy and downmarket — but she had not dreamed that kiss.

'Please,' he whispered, 'at least share a drink with me. Think what a danger I should be on a jet boat if I drank the whole bottle myself.'

Jacq laughed and, shaking her head at her own folly, followed him to the lift. He pressed the button for the Penthouse Suite. She gasped silently. Not only did he have a suite but it was the penthouse itself. The lift stopped one floor below and he pressed again, some secret code that prevented uninvited guests from intruding. As the doors swished open, she gasped again. The luxury was evident. The carpet pile was positively inches thick and the heavy, oak-panelled door opened into a room whose size was quite breathtaking.

He smiled indulgently, beckoning her to the window. He pulled back the blinds so that she could see the lake, shimmering where the lights caught it, the darkness of the mountains making a contrasting backdrop.

'Wow,' she breathed. 'Why would you ever want to leave here?'

'To spend an evening with you. What would you have said if I'd invited you to dinner in my room? You'd have turned me down, and I bet your excuse wouldn't be that you had nothing to wear!'

He slipped his arms round her shoulders and half-turned her towards him. She closed her eyes, waiting for his kiss on her lips. She heard him draw his breath in sharply and looked up at him.

The brown eyes looked misty, a much warmer hue than she'd noticed before.

'I think I'd better get the business out of the way,' he said.

She smiled uncertainly.

'Who exactly are you?' she asked. 'Should I know you?'

She realised that he hadn't told her the whole truth. No ordinary accountant could afford this sort of luxury and with his looks, he might easily have been some film star. The slightly rugged, boy-next-door appeal was always popular with cinema audiences. She racked her brain but couldn't think of a name she could put to the face.

'I'll pour you a drink and then you'll have to excuse me for a moment, while I phone my father,' he said. 'Make yourself comfortable. Won't be long.'

Expertly, he popped the champagne cork and filled the two flutes waiting on the tray. He handed one to her and disappeared into what must be the bedroom.

He must have been pretty sure of

himself, she thought to herself and disliked the doubts that were invading her mind. She sipped the delicious icy champagne. It was a rare treat, saved only for very special occasions at home and then it was only ever the domestic version, not French, like this. She heard a swishing sound, followed by a knock on the big door. Jeb did not appear, so she uncurled herself from the thickly-padded sofa and went to open it. A uniformed butler stood outside, carrying a tray.

'Mr Marlow's order,' he said stiffly.

He came into the room and set the tray down on a side table. He lifted the cover to reveal canapés of smoked salmon and something black and granular that she knew must be caviar. She had never tried caviar but the look of it was not exactly appealing.

'Thank you, ma'am,' he said, bowing slightly as he left the room.

The door shut behind him and the swish of the elevator sounded again.

'Oh, good, the snacks have arrived,'

Jeb said entering the room.

'What did he call you?' she demanded. 'Mr Marlow? What happened to Marsh?'

'Sorry, but it is my only protection when travelling. If I say my name is Marlow, everyone assumes I own the hotels and I get ripped off right, left and centre. People stop treating me as human. Dad hates to travel these days, so I get the job. Hence my anonymity. It's different with the hotel staff, of course. They automatically know when I'm coming and prepare the suite. Have a smoked salmon whatsit.'

Jacq sipped her champagne. What on earth was she doing here, with the heir apparent to a multi-national hotel chain? She took a final swig and put the glass down on the table.

'I have to go,' she mumbled. 'Sorry, Jeb, Mr Marlow.'

She had realised he must have told them to give her her room for some ridiculous price. He had planned it all, just to get her under the same roof. He must think very little of her, if he believed she could be taken in by all that. What was his game? Her cheeks burning, she rushed to the door and pulled it open.

'How do I get the dratted lift up here?' she demanded.

'Wait, Jacq. Please, listen to me.'

'You must think I'm a total fool, an idiot. Perhaps I am but that's no reason for you to take advantage of me.'

'Jacq, Jacquetta, please listen to me. I know what you must be thinking, but I didn't organise anything, well, except the room. I felt I owed you, for being so rotten this morning. But don't you see? I brought you up here because I like you. I wanted to be friends. Dammit! Now you see why I don't broadcast my name. This proves exactly what I mean. You were happy enough to be with me before and now you've let the barriers come between us.'

'I want to go, now,' she insisted, keeping her feelings at bay.

'Please, Jacq. You kissed me in a way

that proved, I mean . . . could mean something to you. Don't spoil it now.'

'You may be used to picking up women for a few days and then dumping them. Whatever you think I am, you've got it wrong. I will not be used by you or anyone else, especially not in return for some cheap hotel room. Now, will you please get that lift up here or I'll . . . I'll have to bungee jump from the window.'

'Now there's a thought,' he said irritatingly. 'It's OK,' he added, seeing the look on her face.

He pressed a switch and the whir of machinery began as the lift rose. Without a word, she went into it and stabbed the buttons to send it down again.

'See you in the morning,' he called.

Jacq leaned back against the lift wall, wishing the awful pounding in her chest would subside. It had been a narrow escape. However much she liked him, however handsome he was, she had no desire to join the long line of his

conquests. The look that the receptionist had given her was a very knowing
one. She didn't fancy having to face
Melissa when she crossed the reception
area. She'd doubtless assume that she
had failed to come up to expectation
and been dismissed. It seemed she had
gone off duty, much to Jacq's relief.

Safely back in her own room, Jacq
scrubbed at her teeth angrily. How
could she have been such a fool? She
would sign out of this hotel, first thing
in the morning. She could afford a
decent room somewhere else. She spat
out the toothpaste, as if she were trying
to spit out the taste of Mr Jeb Marsh
. . . Marlow . . . his champagne and
every bit of his lifestyle with it. How
dare he try to spoil her holiday?

She wouldn't let him spoil anything.
She would have an early breakfast in
the morning and sign out, while he was
still busy having his wretched working
breakfast. Breakfast meetings! What a
poser, she thought. If that was what big
business success meant, you could keep

it. She pulled on her nightshirt and crept into bed. She tossed around, trying to get comfortable.

'Damn Jeb Marsh . . . Marlow,' she whispered, just before she fell into a deep slumber.

Meanwhile, the occupant of the penthouse suite at the Queenstown Marlow was standing gazing out of the window. The tray of canapés lay untouched, alongside the empty glass, abandoned by Jacq. He drained his own glass and poured a second. Pity to waste it, he was thinking. He was tempted by the idea of sending it back to her room but decided against it.

His father had started on again about settling down with some nice girl. His ideas about nice girls and his father's did not coincide at all. He had yet to meet the sort of girl he could really settle down with — someone like Jacquetta would be interesting. But he'd blown that one. All genuinely nice girls were scared off when they discovered who he was.

Jeb drained the glass and put it back on the tray. He paused thoughtfully and decided he would put up a fight for this lady. With luck and a following wind, they could accidentally meet up in several places. He stared up at the ceiling.

He imagined himself wandering round a kiwi fruit orchard, feeding a string of horses with lumps of sugar, while Jacq happily introduced them all by name.

There was nothing he would like more. He might go back to wherever it was she lived and meet her family and the horses she so obviously adored. He tossed and turned over and over in bed.

'Damn Jacquetta Goodman,' he murmured. 'She's got to me,' and eventually, he fell into a fitful sleep.

3

Jacq was up at seven o'clock. Despite being on holiday, the habit of early rising was too deeply ingrained to be broken. She took a shower, dressed, stuffed her few belongings into her hold-all and left the room. She went down to Reception and asked for her bill.

'I'll check out right after breakfast,' she added.

She left her bag in the cloakroom and went up to the luxurious dining-room. She went along the buffet, helping herself to an enormous meal. She had the childish desire to take everything she could, a futile punishment to Jeb for letting her down so badly. She would probably never see him again, but at least she had the comfort of knowing she was in control. She could push him out of her life before her feelings had become involved.

She paid her bill with her credit card, smiling to herself for getting away relatively unscathed. The various desks in the foyer were manned by tour guides and as she had planned to make some excursions, why not make it easy for herself and book here? Jeb would be fully occupied with his precious meeting for some time yet. She booked the jet-boat trip she had talked about. Mr Jeb Marlow was not going to spoil her plans. She still had plenty of time to check into another hotel.

★   ★   ★

'You just have to get out and take pictures here,' the coach driver commanded, halfway through the drive. 'The sun will be lighting those peaks any minute now. Spectacular, isn't it?'

Obediently, they all left the coach and clicked away with cameras, except for Jacq, who hadn't thought to bring hers. She wandered closer to the water's edge, listening to the silence. The water was calm, sheets of glass reflecting the mountains. She watched the ripples, as silver fish leaped out of the water.

'Magnificent, isn't it?' a voice said behind her.

If she hadn't known better, she thought she recognised the cultured, English tones.

'Where on earth did you spring from?' she asked, turning to face Jeb.

'Missed the coach. Had to get a taxi to drop me off here. Knew they always stopped in several places for photos, so I'd easily catch up with you. Smile, please.'

Jeb took her picture with his expensive-looking camera. Then he turned and took another shot, this time of the lake.

Jacq was swept by a whole range of emotions. She felt irritated that he had followed her; pleased to see him again; angry that he had taken for granted she would be happy to see him. All the time her heart was beating wildly, as if trying to contradict whatever her brain was telling her.

'I thought you had a meeting,' she said eventually.

'Been there. Done that,' he said annoyingly. 'Meeting was at seven-thirty. Oh, and I said not to re-let your room today, in case you changed your mind about leaving.'

'You needn't have bothered. I've already checked into another hotel,' she said.

She turned and climbed back on to the bus. Jeb followed her, seating himself beside her.

'Anyone sitting here?' he said loudly, to no-one in particular.

Jacq sat silently, glaring at him whenever he spoke. What gave him the right to follow her?

'I came on this trip to enjoy myself. I won't let you spoil it,' she said coldly.

'I'm here,' he said with a smile, 'to enjoy myself. It didn't take much effort to track down where you'd gone. My receptionist said you'd checked out and also that she'd seen you at the tour desk. Elementary, my dear Goodman.'

The thrills of the jet-boat ride stopped them from further conversation. The innocent-looking boat whizzed along the river, suddenly hurtling straight towards jagged rocks, swerving at the last moment to safer water. They all cried out in terror at first, quickly changing to relieved laughter as they realised the helmsman's strategy. The shallow rocks just below the surface made their hearts pound, looking as though they would slice straight through the rubber craft but they always coasted right over them. If things ever seemed calm, the driver of the boat would give a sudden swoosh round in a complete circle, sending clouds of spray high into the air. It was exciting and very wet.

'What next?' Jeb asked when they returned to dry land.

'I don't know about you but I'm going to try the parapentes, hang-gliding.'

Jeb stared. He couldn't tell whether she was joking or not.

'Are you serious?' he asked at last.

'Never more so,' she said, perhaps half-hoping he'd try to talk her out of it.

'Fine,' he said. 'Me, too.'

She stared at him.

'Are you serious?' she asked.

'Never more so,' he echoed.

He hoped she hadn't noticed the slight gulp in his throat as he spoke. He really couldn't think of anything he'd hate more, bungee jumping apart, but he was determined that he was going to stay firmly by her side for the whole day. Although she had considered trying the tandem hang-glider, she had never intended to do it. She knew she was testing Jeb's courage, though it was a relatively safe exercise. Now, unless she was to go back on her word, she was committed to it.

If she could have seen into Jeb's mind, she would have been amused at the consternation she had caused. He could never have admitted that he was plain scared and was looking for an excuse to get out of it. He couldn't claim a meeting or prior appointment, not when he'd boasted of clearing his day to spend it with her.

Jacq led the way to the booking office. Jeb's face was set firm in his efforts to hide his real feelings. They pushed the door open and Jacq led the way in.

'Hi, there. We'd like to do the parapentes, if possible. Soon as we can.'

To his immense relief, the girl said they had cancelled all jumps for the rest of the day, due to high winds.

'Oh, what a shame,' he said just a trifle too quickly.

'You could book for tomorrow if you like. The forecast's good,' she offered.

'What do you think, darling?' Jeb asked, his contrived familiarity irritating her.

'No use. I shall be leaving first thing in the morning. Thanks anyway.'

She turned and walked out of the

office, leaving a bewildered Jeb, standing with his mouth open. He shrugged and raised his hands to the girl behind the desk and followed Jacq out into the street.

'Wait, Jacq. What do you mean, you're leaving in the morning?'

'Should have thought that was pretty obvious. I've had enough of holidaying. I'm going home,' she replied and strode off.

'Since when?' he demanded, chasing after her.

'Since right now. I don't know why you're hounding me, Jeb. I thought I'd made it quite clear that I am not interested, not now, not ever. Please just get out of my life.'

'I'm glad you care so much. I do, too. Shall we drive back together?'

'How do you mean, drive?'

'You said you were going to drive, to see the country at ground level. I'd be pleased to offer you a seat in my car. You can share the driving if you like. I expect you drive as well as you fly.'

She shook her head in disbelief. What did she have to do to get rid of him? He may be drop dead gorgeous and richer than Midas himself, but he was self-opinionated, self-satisfied . . .

'I've decided to fly after all,' she announced.

'Fine by me,' he said, annoyingly. 'Which flight are you on?'

'Don't know yet.'

'I'll ask Melissa to get us two tickets, shall I? I don't suppose you usually travel first class, do you?'

'I usually fly myself,' she retorted. 'Besides, internal flights here are usually classless. I'll sort myself out, thanks. I'm going back to my hotel now, so I'll say goodbye.'

She walked away from him, leaving him standing gazing after her. He had an odd little smile on his face, one which might have disconcerted her, had she seen it.

At her new hotel, the receptionist handed Jacq a typed message. The woman looked uncomfortable as Jacq ripped open the envelope.

'Just what does this mean?' she asked.

'The manager regrets, but he is unable to offer you accommodation after all.'

Her voice was clipped and she was clearly embarrassed.

'I want to see him, right now.'

'I'm afraid he is not available, madam. I should be grateful if you would take your luggage and leave.'

'But this is a complete lie. I did pay my bill at Marlow's Hotel. I have a receipt for it. Look, here it is.'

She pulled the crumpled paper from her bag and showed the woman, who smiled superciliously.

'You may have paid for your breakfast but this hardly includes a room, not at the Marlow. I'm sorry, but they warned us that you might try the same trick here. Please, leave now, before I am obliged to call the police . . . '

The cold, sick feeling settled in the pit of her stomach. That man had set her up. If he didn't get what he wanted, he really knew how to play it dirty. If that was what money did for you, she'd rather be poor. If Jeb Marlow thought she would go back there cap in hand, he had another think coming. She stamped out of the hotel and went to the bank where she cashed a cheque. If he tried the same trick again, he'd be disappointed. With a cash customer, it became irrelevant.

There was a huge, old boat moored at the quay. *The Earnslaw*, the sign read. *Evening cruises with a traditional dinner at Walter's Peak Sheep Station.* If she went on that trip, Jeb Marlow would never know where she was and she could spend a peaceful evening looking at someone else's farm. She might even pick up some ideas for their place. All that was left to do was to organise her flight home.

Using her contacts, she arranged a flight to Wellington and knew she could organise another flight back home from there. Amazing where you could go when you knew folks with their own planes.

At least she could avoid Jeb's company for the journey. It was a pity they had to be from such opposite worlds. He had everything she could ever have wanted in a man — sense of humour, good company, wonderful looks. But he was too used to getting his own way, whatever the cost to anyone else. It was a paradox that his one failing was his fantastic wealth, and no real independence.

It seemed he was at his father's beck and call. Besides, she could never fit in with the sort of company he was obviously used to. She could imagine endless rounds of boring dinner parties with business clients. His wife would always have to be immaculate and well-groomed. Jacq could never be bothered with all that. For her, life was for spending with people you loved, doing things you enjoyed. Hours spent at hairdressers, dressmakers or beauty parlours were definitely not on her list.

All the same, it had been flattering that he wanted to spend time with her.

She wandered back and impulsively went into one of the boutiques and bought herself a light olive green trouser suit. It cost far more than she usually paid for practical clothes, but it fitted so exactly and the colour suited her perfectly, it gave her confidence a much-needed boost.

Later, aboard the Earnslaw, dressed in her new suit, Jacq leaned over the rail of the boat, listening to the deep chugging of the old steam engine as it ploughed across the lake. The sun was still warm and sent patches of light shimmering over the water. Some sixth sense told her there was someone standing behind her. Knowing it was Jeb, she turned, feigning anger as she faced him.

'I suppose you are going to tell me that the receptionist phoned every tour possible to see if I was on it?'

'Naturally. Melissa is the perfect employee. Does everything I want.'

'I bet she does,' Jacq said sarcastically.

'Don't spoil a glorious evening,' Jeb said softly. 'Pretend you just met me for the first time and let's take it from there.'

'And in this scenario, do you lie about your identity or are you Honest Jeb from the start?'

'What a woman! Peace, anything. Let's enjoy the scenery and the evening. You look great. That colour is definitely you.'

Despite herself, Jacq smiled.

'Thanks,' she said, relenting. 'OK. Peace it is. Can I buy you a drink?'

He stared at her, about to protest but suddenly, his face crumpled into a huge grin that sent her heart careering through a series of crashes and whirls that were quite uncontrollable.

'I'll have a beer, thanks.'

He was learning. She went below to the bar, to order the drinks.

At the Walter's Peak Farm, there were displays of sheepdogs and various animals to pet, followed by a homely, filling meal.

'I shall put on the pounds if I carry on eating like this,' Jacq said. 'I don't know when I've ever eaten so much or so often.'

'You'll soon lose it when you're back working. Now, how about a walk down by the lake, before we have to leave?'

He slipped his arm around her waist, pulling her close to him as they walked. Despite herself, she couldn't help but allow it. She felt the same thrill of anticipation as the previous night. Only this time, she was firmly in control. If only it weren't all so complicated. Most people could settle for a quick holiday fling and enjoy every moment. Why on earth couldn't she feel like that? Blast her stubborn pride. Perhaps the holiday fling wasn't usually with the son of a family who owned squillions.

Almost as if he could read her mind, he said, 'It's OK. I'm not pushing my luck. You made your position clear last night. But I like you a lot. I enjoy your company and I sense that you enjoy mine. Friends?'

'Yes, friends, but I still don't understand. Why me? You could have the pick of practically anyone you wanted. Models, film stars even.'

'Perhaps that's it. I'm sick of glossy model types. You are real, beautiful and completely honest.'

She stared at him. She wondered if she could believe what he was saying.

On the return journey, the temperature was considerably cooler, as the darkness fell around them. Jeb slipped his jacket off and put it round Jacq's shoulders, so they could stay up on the deck. She whispered her thanks and snuggled into it.

'I'll walk you to your hotel,' he offered. 'Where are you staying now?'

'You mean your efficient Melissa didn't manage to find that out? Oh, yes, I'd forgotten that rotten trick you pulled. That was really below the belt.'

How could she have forgotten about it all evening? She had intended never to have anything more to do with him after that. It all went to prove his power over her and how ineffectual she was. Jeb Marlow was a difficult bloke to get rid of.

'I am really sorry. I couldn't bear the thought of not seeing you again. I admit, it was a rotten trick. Desperate men do desperate things.' He smiled. 'I hoped you would come back to the Marlow. Forgive me?'

'As I probably won't ever have to see you again, I suppose.'

'What time do you leave tomorrow?' he asked. 'I could come and see you off if you'll allow it.'

Jacq paused. Did she really want to see him again? The friend she was hitching a ride with wouldn't have room for Jeb as well, so it was probably safe to allow him to come to the airport. True to his word, he said good-night with a simple peck on the cheek.

'If only,' she whispered to herself, as she lay in her bed.

She wondered why she had to be so stupid, when most other women would have leaped at the chance of a real relationship with him. But, she was not most other women. She remained convinced that Jeb Marlow was simply amusing himself at her expense.

Her stained, ancient travel bag looked quite out of place in the huge limo that swept her to the airport next morning. The uniformed driver had a mask of indifference as he stowed her bag on the seat beside him. Jeb sat next to Jacq in the rear.

'Thought it would be easier if I didn't have to drive and then find somewhere to park,' he said.

'You mean you thought you'd have one final go at impressing me,' she chided but his grin was almost boyish in its innocence.

'How about a glass of wine?' he offered, pushing a lever to reveal a small bar. 'There's a nice dry white I can offer, or you might like something stronger?'

'Jeb, it is eight o'clock in the morning. I am about to fly out of here in a small plane. It may be part of your lifestyle but I do not drink alcohol of any kind at this time of day, not in any circumstances.'

'Ouch,' he winced. 'Just thought I'd offer.'

She glared, the faint twitching at the corners of her mouth giving away her real thoughts.

'This is it then,' Jacq announced as they pulled up in front of the airport building.

'Does it have to be? The shortest romance ever, from one airport to another.'

His voice held a note of sadness but Jacq doubted its sincerity.

'I'm afraid so. But I'd hardly call it a romance, would you?'

'I guess I'm thinking of what might have been. You're different, a very special lady.'

'Come on now. You'll forget all about me by the end of the day. This was just

67

a fling, to you at least. I'm going back to my own world now. My world is simple, remote and dammed hard work. You are used to whizzing round the entire globe, the best of everything to ease it along. That's all 'way out of my league. Your life is champagne. Mine is kiwi fruit. Thanks for the lift and have a nice life.'

Jeb stared after her retreating figure, clad in black leather flying gear. She looked about fifteen again, her hair done up in its pony tail. What was it about her that infuriated him, excited him and made him want more and more of her? He ordered the driver to return him to his hotel, realising this town held no further interest for him. Where was she flying to? Wellington? He dialled the reception desk on his mobile.

'Get me the next available flight to Wellington, and while you're doing that, get someone to do my packing.'

He snapped the phone shut and dropped it back in his pocket.

* ★ ★

Jacq and Mick, her pilot, had known
each other for years. He ferried cargo
and passengers wherever they wanted
to go, usually within New Zealand.
They reminisced as much as the noise
of the plane allowed them. Mick had
two kids and a wife he adored, living
just outside Wellington. He persuaded
Jacq to go back home with him.

'Marie would love to see you again
and she'd be glad of another female to
talk to. Gets sick of just me and the
kids,' he said.

'OK, Thanks, you're on. They're not
expecting me back home for a while
yet. Be good to have time to talk again.
Can you radio through to cancel my
onward ticket?'

She had cleared the airport on
arrival, 'way before the next Air New
Zealand flight had even landed. Jeb
scanned every corner of the terminal,
even waiting outside the Ladies, in case
she was in there. He went to the

check-in desk and using all his consid-erable charm, discovered Jacq had cancelled her onward flight. He marched angrily to the bar and ordered himself a large whisky. She had done it deliberately. Well, he didn't give up so easily. He would go to Rotorua and stay there for a few days. Melissa, or her equivalent in the Rotorua Marlow, could do some research for him. Miss Jacquetta Goodman had met her match and the sooner she realised it, the better.

It was four days later when Jacq finally returned home. Her sister hugged her.

'Gosh, I've missed your ugly face and bad temper.' She laughed.

'What's to miss? You only have to look in the mirror,' she retorted. 'Same face. Shame about the temper though!'

The two girls were indeed mirror images of each other, physically at least. Their temperaments couldn't have been more different. Jamylla was calm, even-tempered and hated any sort of aggression. When they had been children, it had always been Jamie who had given way, anything to stop her fiery sister from shouting or arguing.

'That's what I like to see, both my girls back home.'

Peter Goodman stood leaning on the door frame, his tall, angular figure almost filling it.

'Hi, Dad. You miss me?' Jacq said as she went to hug him.

'Missed the noise,' he teased. 'Been too peaceful without the pair of you scrapping.'

Jacq grinned. It was good to be home.

'Horses OK?' she asked.

'Perry cast a shoe, Jasmin's been unmanageable without you but apart from that, nothing much has happened. Oh, and we've suddenly been plagued with phone calls but they hang up every time.'

Jacq's heart missed a beat. He couldn't! Jeb couldn't have got her number. No, she was letting her imagination run wild. It was exactly what Jamie said, someone trying to do a spot of cold calling. She had surely seen the last of Mr Jeb Marlow.

She changed into her old working jeans and the two girls went out to the paddock. Her pockets filled with peppermints, Jacq was soon being nuzzled by the herd of ponies.

'Cupboard love.' She laughed, enjoying the feel and smell of the friendly animals. 'Let's go for a ride. I need some good, clean air.'

The twins shared their love of horses and the open country and were soon galloping over the fields, between the high rows of trees, planted to provide shelter belts for the kiwi orchards.

'How are they coming on?' Jacq asked, when they had slowed down to walking pace, nodding towards the fruit vines.

'Doing well, Dad says.'

Neither of the girls had much to do with the fruit growing, as they were usually kept busy with the horses, riding lessons and the pony treks. Jacq smiled ruefully, thinking of Jeb Marlow and his frantic dashing round the world. Despite his wealth, she felt sorry for him. He had never really known the love and security of a real family.

Jacq's thoughts kept straying to Jeb. The memory of the kiss they had shared, at the edge of Lake Wakatipu sent rushes of heat coursing through her body. She tried to push away all thoughts of him. He was a rich playboy and no-one in their right mind could believe he was interested in some small town girl from the sticks. He was used to smart, sophisticated women.

She rode high among the hills surrounding their land, at ease among the tree-ferns and pines. This was where she belonged, not among posh hotels and champagne lifestyles.

⋆   ⋆   ⋆

Jeb drove into the yard outside the long, low farmhouse. He had hired a powerful car, which had quickly lapped up the miles from Rotorua and he had arrived earlier than he'd expected. He walked to the door, wondering about his reception. He was about to ring the bell when he saw her, standing looking over the paddock rail. She wore pale blue denim jeans, rolled up at the bottom and a check shirt. So this was Jacq in her home domain. He liked the sight and walked over to her.

'Before you say a word, I want you to hear me out,' he began.

The girl swung round, startled by his voice.

'I couldn't leave without seeing you again. Besides, I have an idea, a business idea I'd like to discuss.'

'What sort of business?' she asked, hardly seeming to show a flicker of surprise at his appearance.

'A contract for you to supply the hotels with fresh fruit and vegetables. We have three hotels in this area alone and if we can work it out, it could guarantee a ready market for anything you can produce.'

'I see. Sounds like an offer we can't refuse,' she replied.

'And you're not mad at me for tracking you down?'

'Why should I be?'

'I just thought you might be. You have something of a temper, as I found out to my cost.'

'I never have a temper,' the girl said honestly.

'OK, OK. The last thing I want is to argue.'

He put his hand tentatively on her arm. As she didn't make any indication that she was unhappy with it, he chanced his luck again and slipped it across her shoulder in a familiar gesture.

'I've missed you,' he whispered.

'So it seems,' Jamie replied, with a mischievous grin.

4

'Come and have dinner with me,' Jeb said suddenly. 'We have a lot to talk about. Come on. Let's go right now. We'll drive somewhere quiet, just the two of us and start all over again.'

'Sounds wonderful,' Jamie said sweetly, much to Jeb's consternation.

It was not the response he had been expecting — Jacq giving in without a fight? Whatever had happened in the time since they had met? She almost seemed to be a different person. But he shouldn't complain. Things were looking distinctly more promising. Now she was safely back in her own environment, she was much more at ease, less prickly but certainly no less beautiful. He had not been mistaken about that.

'Do you know somewhere special to eat around here?' Jeb asked.

'Depends what sort of place you're

looking for. Cash, cheque book or credit card?'

'Only the best. I thought you'd remember that much at least!'

He was almost ready to risk kissing her, when he heard a voice, a very familiar voice.

'What in heaven's name are you doing here? And what are you doing with your arm round my sister?'

Jeb leaped away from Jamie, his mouth open in shock and astonishment.

'Jacq? Good heavens!' He stared at the two of them and shook his head. 'Amazing. Two of you. I've never seen two people looking so incredibly alike.'

'Meet my sister. Jamie, this is Jeb Marlow, of Marlow Hotels. Don't be fooled though. He lives in a different world to anyone we've ever known.'

'Pleased to meet you, Jamie,' he said softly. 'I thought Jacq was being rather more polite than usual. Now I can understand why, and, yes, my father owns the Marlow Hotels but I only work for him. You shouldn't believe I'm anything other than an ordinary man.'

'Who travels everywhere first-class and lives in penthouse suites,' Jacq responded almost snappily, feeling irrationally jealous of the arm that was still resting on Jamie's shoulder.

'Well, it seems that dinner invitation should be extended to both of you,' Jeb said with a smile. 'Every man's fantasy, I guess. Two identical beautiful women.'

'Jamie's busy this evening, aren't you?'

'Well, I . . . yes. I'm probably seeing Matt.'

'Are you always this calm? You're certainly less prickly than your sister.'

'I'll say. I'm the hearthside kitten to her tiger.' Jamie laughed.

'I deny it all,' Jacq called out. 'I'm an absolute pussycat myself.'

'Just a matter of deciding which type of pussycat,' Jeb said wryly.

Jacq moved closer to him, gently disengaging his arm from her sister.

'So what are you doing here anyway?

I certainly never expected to see you again.'

'As I was saying to your good-tempered sister here, I have a business proposition for you, fruit, vegetables. We have quite a demand with our hotels around here. Good for our guests to enjoy local produce. I could probably take most of what you can produce.'

Jeb had swung into business mode.

'We only handle the riding side,' Jacq said. 'You'd have to talk to Dad. He's somewhere around. Now, if you'll excuse me, I have things to do.'

'How did you two meet? Spill the beans. I know you, Jacq. You only act this dumb when you're interested in someone.'

Jamie stared at her sister, frowning just slightly.

'Besides, you need to get ready for dinner. He's taking you somewhere really special. No expense spared.'

'I believe it was you he asked,' Jacq snapped.

'Excuse me,' Jeb interrupted. 'Do I get a say in any of this?'

'That depends on Jamie.'

Jacq swept in through the screen door of the house. Jamie looked uncomfortable. Jeb had a tiny gleam of irritation in his steely eyes but a smile played at the corners of his mouth. This was more like the Jacquetta he remembered.

'I'm sorry my sister was so rude. Perhaps she was simply surprised at seeing you so unexpectedly,' Jamie tried to pacify him.

'I'm sure she meant every word of it. It wouldn't be Jacq to give in without a struggle.'

'You obviously know her well,' Jamie remarked. 'I'm sure she'll come round. Why not take a look at the farm and come back later? Half an hour or so should do it.'

It was amazing that two people who looked so alike could be so different in character. He'd always believed that identical twins were identical in every way, but already, he was beginning to know better.

He looked around. Everywhere was clean and immaculately tidy but the out-buildings were old and patched with sheets of corrugated iron. It was obvious that this family had kept things going by sheer hard work, just to make ends meet. A decent-sized contract could make all the difference to them.

'Look, I'm not trying to hold anything over either of you, but I could help with a decent contract. Can I talk to your father? We could all benefit, the hotels with good-quality fresh produce and you would have a guaranteed income each month.'

Jeb was business-like and Jamie instinctively liked this good-looking stranger who seemed to be more than a little interested in her volatile sister.

'Dad's somewhere out in the fields. Have a wander round. Introduce yourself to him. He's sure to invite you back for tea, so I'll go and put the kettle on.'

Jeb turned and walked down the paddock towards the vegetable field. Jamie watched him, the tall, angular figure striding uncompromisingly over the lush green turf. He was a man who knew what he wanted. She wondered why her sister was so aggressive towards him. Jacq had said little about her trip. The two girls usually told each other everything, especially about boyfriends.

When Jamie had finally fallen in love with Matt, a neighbouring farmer, it had been with Jacq's total approval. It was a perfect match, she had said, and now the pair were planning to get engaged, once the picking season was over. Jamie felt hurt that her twin had not confided in her this time. Perhaps it was a sign that they were finally growing apart. She went inside, hearing Jacq splashing noisily in the shower. She was singing tunelessly, as if trying to show how little she cared about any good-looking male who happened to be visiting the farm.

'So, spill the beans on your tame

hunk,' Jamie demanded once Jacq emerged from the shower.

'He isn't mine and he certainly isn't tame,' she snapped.

'But you have to admit to the hunk description. He's gorgeous.'

'I admit to nothing.'

She carried on drying herself, apparently unconcerned.

'Oh, all right. I flew him, or tried to fly him up from the South. It was misty and I had to go back. We ended up taking the bus together. End of story.'

'Whoa, there. There's much more between you two than a few hours' bus ride. I could practically see the electricity flying between you.'

'Rubbish,' Jacq protested, staring in disbelief. 'OK. He took me for dinner but when payment included a full-blown seduction routine in his penthouse, I told him I was not for sale.'

Jamie burst out laughing.

'So you really are keen. I thought as much,' she added, but her smile faded as Jacq looked as if she might burst into tears.

'Sorry, love, I didn't mean to make fun. You really like him?'

Jamie's voice was gentle.

'Oh, Jamie, I thought he might be someone special. Like you said, he is gorgeous but so stinking rich, it puts him right out of my league. He's fun and good company, but not for me. He's probably got a woman waiting in every town in the world. He's used to penthouse suites, champagne all the way and dainty snacks of smoked salmon and caviar. Hereabouts, it's steak and piles of veggies, not to mention the dreaded kiwi fruit. We come from totally different worlds.'

'Don't you think you may be judging him a little harshly? I mean, he did seek you out, all the way out here. Think about it.'

'He needed some produce for his precious hotels,' Jacq continued.

'He could buy that anywhere. Why bother to come all the way here, if he didn't want to see you?'

'I guess he must have got the impression that we were struggling a bit to make a go of things.'

'There you are then. He likes you and came here to do us all a good turn.'

'We're not some charity case,' Jacq snapped. 'No, I tell you. He's 'way out of my league. I could never fit into his world, not in a million years.'

'He's coming into the house right now, with Dad. They look as though they are chatting quite happily. We'd better go down.'

With a glare, Jacq pulled on a clean pair of jeans and followed her sister down the stairs. Jeb was leaning lazily against the kitchen counter, chatting to their father like an old friend. Jamie put the kettle on as Jeb was staring, as if trying to work out which of the sisters it was.

'Can you tell which is which?' he asked Peter.

'Mostly. But they delight in giving out wrong messages and confusing anyone and everyone. Jacq's temper is usually the first to go.'

'That I can believe.' Jeb laughed. 'So, Jamie, has Jacq relented? Is she going to have dinner with me?'

Jamie shrugged as her sister came into the room.

'This young man's been telling me about his plans for the hotels,' Pete said with a note of warning in his voice. 'Says he could do a deal for us to supply fresh fruit and veg. Make all the difference to us. I hope you'll discuss it with him over dinner, Jacq.'

Jacq looked at the two men and smiled sweetly.

'Of course, Daddy, but he must realise that this is purely business and I am not part of any deal you cook up between you.'

Inside, she was seething. How dared they compromise her like this? To refuse Jeb's invitation looked as if it might jeopardise a much-needed business deal but as far as he was concerned, presumably, she came with the deal.

The man was unscrupulous and obviously willing to go to any lengths to get what he wanted. She knew instinctively that he could only be interested in her because she had turned him down. If she relaxed once, he would surely dump her just as quickly. Men like Jeb Marlow could never be serious about an unsophisticated girl from a remote kiwi farm.

'Aren't you going to get ready?' Jamie asked when they had finished tea.

Sulkily, Jacq went upstairs and looked into her limited wardrobe. Jamie followed her and began to pull out various garments for her inspection. They argued for several minutes.

'I never wear skirts,' Jacq grumbled. 'Look, why don't you go out with him? You always make a good impression. Pretend you're me and get the deal settled, for Dad's sake.'

'And do I allow him to kiss me? If he wants to, that is,' Jamie teased.

Jacq looked down at her nails, as if inspecting them in great detail. Never wanting to admit to it, she felt a surge of jealousy at the thought. She needed to dispel such thoughts. She should never allow herself to feel any jealousy, not where a man like Jeb was concerned. All the same, she couldn't bear the thought of Jeb kissing anyone else, even if he did think it was her.

'OK, I'll go, but it's for Dad's sake. He deserves some good luck.'

'Fine. You might even enjoy yourself at the same time. Now, get yourself ready and borrow whatever you need.'

Jacq turned back to their wardrobes and grumpily pulled out various things. Why did she never have the right clothes for anything? She took out a floaty skirt of Jamie's and found a T-shirt that was a reasonable match. Identical though the sisters were, she always thought of her twin as the pretty, feminine one and herself as the tomboy. She felt as if things were getting out of control and she didn't like it. All the same, her heart did very peculiar things when she saw him sitting quite relaxed at the kitchen table in their rather scruffy kitchen.

'Hi,' she said, slightly hesitant. 'Hope I'll do.'

'You look fine to me,' Jeb said with a grin.

He glanced back at Jamie and Jacq once more sensed a rush of jealousy. Perhaps he would rather go out with her sister. She took a deep breath, promising herself that she would try hard to make the evening a success. Thinking about that brief stay in Queenstown was enough to rekindle a whole range of emotions. But whatever happened, she told herself, it was only temporary. She could enjoy his company but she must never allow herself to have any sort of feelings about him. It was doomed to failure and she would be hurt.

'Let's go then. I'll warn you, I'm ravenous and this evening is going to cost you a whole packet of money.'

'Jacquetta!' her father protested. 'Really. What will Mr Marlow think of us?'

She gave a wicked grin as she bounced out of the door.

'Don't often see Jacquetta in a skirt, do we?' Jamie said to her dad and raised one eyebrow with a smile.

It was a pleasant evening and despite all her own warnings, Jacq relaxed and enjoyed the company of her good-looking escort. He really was fun and they sparked off something in each other that made them seem like old friends. He smiled as she ate her way through three large courses, washed down with some of the local good wine. She leaned back and sighed in satisfaction.

'Anything else for madame?' Jeb asked but she shook her head. 'I've got something to ask you. A business proposition,' he went on.

'Oh, yes. Consider you've softened me up sufficiently?'

'I hope so. How would you feel about flying me around a bit? I have to visit several of the hotels in the next few days and it would save me so much time if we could charter a small plane and you took me to the various places. I'd be looking at a few days, that's all. I thought your friend, Hal, would probably hire us his plane.'

'I couldn't leave the farm for that long. We have all sorts of commitments.'

'I don't think that would be a problem. Your father and sister seem to think they can manage.'

'You've discussed this with them, before you'd even asked me?'

'Well, I was just testing the ground. See if they thought it was feasible, and it is.'

'Always assuming I am willing to give up my time.'

'I was intending to pay you. I'm not asking for any favours.'

A smile twitched at the corners of his mouth.

'Just as well. Assuming Hal is willing to hire out his plane, when were you thinking of?'

'Tomorrow, preferably.'

'Heavens! I'm not sure if there's time to cover all the paperwork and organise everything else.'

She felt torn between the opportunity to fly for several days and her own need to distance herself from this powerful man who was driving her crazy, if she admitted it. Whole days spent in his company could all be just too much.

'I suppose I could give Hal a call first thing in the morning.'

'No need. I already spoke to him. The Cessna's ours if we want it. I gave him a rough list of places I need to visit and he was putting it all together for us.'

'You take a lot for granted, don't you? What if I'd said no?'

'I never thought you would, but, if you had turned down my offer, I could always hire another pilot.'

'Jeb Marlow, you have to be one of the most irritating men I have ever met.'

'So it's a yes? You'll fly me all over this beautiful island of yours?'

'I suppose.'

He reached over the table and took her hand. She tensed and tried to pull it away. He held on tight until he felt her relax and gave her fingers a gentle squeeze. Immediately she became tense again.

'Relax. I'm merely conveying my thanks. If keeping me at arm's length is what you want, that's fine. It isn't what I want, but I'll respect your wishes.'

Jacq contemplated him again. He was almost too good to be true. Why did she have to be so suspicious of him?

'I'm sorry,' she said. 'I just don't want any complications. You may be here right now and dangling all sorts of fantastic offers to us but you'll be off again in a few days. If we keep it businesslike, it won't hurt so much when you go.'

'Now that sounds suspiciously like an admission of feelings,' Jeb said, a wide grin on his face. 'And to think I almost asked Jamie to come out this evening instead of you. Thought she seemed a much gentler soul altogether.'

'And to think I was trying to persuade Jamie to go out with you instead of me. We'd probably have got away with it, too.'

'Never. I'd have known the instant I kissed her. Now, shall we go? We have a busy day ahead of us tomorrow. I'll pick you up around eleven-thirty. Just pack the essentials. We can always get anything else you might need at one of the hotel boutiques.'

'I'd hate to embarrass you by not wearing the correct clothes, so don't expect me to be dining with you in posh places. I'm just a country hick at heart, don't forget.'

5

Jamie and Pete were waiting for Jacq's return. She outlined her plans and made sure they really were going to manage without her for the next few days. There were a couple of pony treks booked but Jamie was certain she would manage. Pete assured her that he would call in extra help for the veggies if needed but he, too, was sure they could manage.

'He's offered me a generous fee for the trip so you can use that to buy any extra help you need,' Jacq told them. 'Now I must get some sleep. 'Night.'

She felt exhausted and even confessed that she felt disappointed that Jeb hadn't tried to kiss her. She could hardly blame him after all that had been said but she still felt some regrets. A few days in his exclusive company could make quite a difference.

As Jacq taxied across the runway at the little airfield on the day of their departure, she felt the thrill of power and rush of adrenalin as the plane lifted off the ground. She would never tire of that particular excitement. She glanced at Jeb and saw his lips pressed hard together. He was far from relaxed but he was never going to admit to it.

She remembered the look on his face on their previous flight and realised how much it had cost him in stress to undertake this journey. She couldn't help wonder at his motives for putting himself through it. Just to be with her, she wondered. He could have his pick of any woman, anywhere. He was rich and good looking, a catch for anyone.

She spoke into the lip mike and cleared the airfield, setting course for Lake Taupo, a relatively short flight. Jeb had arranged, as with all his stops, for a local car to pick him up, to take him directly to make his calls. Jacq would stay with the aircraft to refuel when necessary and do anything else she needed. She quickly realised that she would have long periods of time to kill and planned to buy herself a good book at the first opportunity. Following his stay there, they were moving farther down the west coast to stay overnight.

They finally reached New Plymouth early in the evening. Jacq had been given a staff room and she sat down on the bed feeling totally exhausted. The waiting around had been tedious but never restful. Flying planes isn't all glamour, she muttered to herself. She showered and changed into her new green outfit and went down to dinner, as arranged, with Jeb.

He seemed relaxed and told her something of the business he was involved in. His father had come up with the idea of having an approved range of family homes which would offer the genuine New Zealand experience to tourists. Jeb was looking into the possibility of a chain of them, near enough to the hotels to offer an extra choice to their guests.

Jacq thought it sounded like a good idea and even began to wonder if they might offer such accommodation themselves, not without a great deal of expensive changes to the property, she decided ruefully. Jeb once more behaved impeccably and never once made her feel defensive. She almost began to think she had been imagining any attraction she had felt or thought he had felt.

'Let's have some champagne on my balcony,' he said suddenly.

'I couldn't, thank you. I've got to keep a clear head for flying tomorrow and we had wine with dinner.'

'So what? We can always stay over another day, see some sights. We can use the boat to explore a bit of the coast, relax a bit.'

'I'm sorry, Jeb. I really do have to get back home by the weekend. I have work to do. I told you, I'm just not used to the champagne lifestyle. What's the boat, anyhow?'

'Just a sailing boat. Seaworthy, of course.'

He didn't say any more about it but she could well believe it was probably some huge yacht, complete with full crew. She sighed gently as she shook her head. He simply took so much for granted. She could never take even a few days off without a great deal of planning and organising. However hard he worked, Jeb was still largely his own boss, living in luxury and taking advantage of facilities wherever he happened to be — and what facilities. She'd simply never cope with quite so much affluence.

The next couple of days passed in a whirl of flying to various places, some of them remote with only a small landing strip near the property. Jacq enjoyed it immensely and even admitted to herself that she enjoyed Jeb's company more than any other male she had met. Dear old Hal had never come anywhere near him in any way.

On the final evening of their trip,

they stayed in a small hotel near to a wonderful cave complex.

'Don't tell me you've never visited Waitomo?' she asked Jeb in some disbelief.

For someone who had been everywhere, it was good to find she knew of something he didn't.

'Come on then. There's just about time before they close.'

They spent an hour wandering round the spectacular caves with huge stalagmites and stalactites, forming alien shapes, dominating the surroundings. They saw glow worms, thousands of them, lighting the ceilings like some exotic light display.

'Quite amazing. Why didn't I know about this place? Makes a superb attraction for anyone staying here. Countryside around here isn't bad either.'

He pulled out his notebook and scribbled some details. Jacq sighed. He saw everything with an eye for the business potential.

'Just see it all for its own sake for once,' she said irritably.

'Let's go and find some dinner. Then we'll fly back first thing. You should be back with your precious horses soon after lunch.'

'I hope Jamie managed the trek OK. Matt said he'd go with her but he's not as experienced as I am.'

'Phone them. Let them know you'll be back tomorrow, if it will allow you to relax and enjoy our last evening together.'

'I think I might.'

Jeb handed her his mobile.

'Go on. Use it.'

'I can use the public phone. It'll be cheaper.'

'Don't be ridiculous. Go on.'

She punched in the number and waited. She got the answering machine.

'Hi. Only me, just to say I'll be back tomorrow. Where are you all? Thought you'd be eating supper by now. See you tomorrow.'

She switched off the phone and frowned.

101

'That's odd. They're never out this late. It's practically dark, so they'll hardly be out on the farm.'

'Maybe they've gone out for the evening. Dinner out, or visiting neighbours.'

'Dad never eats out. Reckons it's a waste of money. And we don't have neighbours, not ones we visit with.'

'Cheer up. This is the last time you'll have to put up with me, for a while, at least.'

'I've enjoyed it. Thanks for asking me. I'm starving. Shall we eat here or in town?'

After a large and healthy meal they took a final stroll down near the water. It was still warm and the sky was speckled with stars.

'There's the Southern Cross,' Jacq pointed.

Jeb rested his arm on her shoulder as he looked up. She tried to ignore the closeness of him and his maleness. His hand slid along her shoulder and he turned her face towards him. His kiss

102

was gentle, every bit as thrilling as she remembered.

'Please, Jeb. I may not be able to turn you away if you keep doing that.'

'Exactly what I was hoping. Why do you always have to push me away? I thought you liked me, enjoyed my company.'

'I do, but I shouldn't. As I keep pointing out to you, you live in a different world to mine. I could never cope with your world. I love my home, my family, my work. Besides, you would never be with me for long, and you must meet dozens of women, all much more your sort of people than I could ever be. Besides, I don't want to get hurt,' she finished lamely.

'Why would I ever hurt you? Jacquetta, you are beautiful! You're fun, loyal. I enjoy being with you. I'd like us to be more than friends. Please, don't push me away.'

'I'm too scared not to. Come on, let's go back. We can make an early start in the morning and then you won't have to put up with me any more either.'

Jeb sighed and let her go. What was wrong with him?

Just as they arrived back at their hotel, Jeb's mobile phone rang.

'Yes? She's right here. It's your father.'

He handed the phone to her and she put it to her ear.

'Hi, Dad. Is something wrong?' She paused, listening. 'Oh, no,' she gasped. 'Is she all right? Oh, heavens. Oh, Dad, poor Jamie. Yes. Yes, tomorrow morning, as soon as we possibly can. Should I go straight to Tauranga? OK. No, I'm sure Jeb won't mind. See you tomorrow. Try to get some sleep.'

'What's happened?' Jeb asked anxiously.

'Jamie's had an accident. I knew I shouldn't have left her to cope. It was far too much for her to do on her own.'

'How bad is it?'

'They don't know. She's in hospital, of course. They're doing tests but there's a definite possibility that she

104

might never walk again.'

As she spoke, the tears were running freely down her cheeks until finally, she broke down completely, clinging to Jeb's supporting body. His arms held her tightly, comforting and giving her strength.

'I said we'd go straight to Tauranga in the morning. You can always get transport back to Rotorua. I can try to organise a flight for you if you like. It isn't that long a drive, though.'

Her voice was broken with sobs.

'Hush, my love,' Jeb whispered. 'Don't worry about it. I'll be with you. We can go at first light. Don't worry about me. You must try to get some rest now.'

'To think I was trailing you round the caves with no thought of anything else and all the time poor Jamie was lying in hospital. I just don't know how we'll manage if she . . . she can't walk again. I can't bear it. Why did I have to be away?'

'Stop it. It isn't your fault. It could

105

just as well have happened when you were there. Now, bed for you, young lady. I'll order some cocoa for you and a large brandy. No arguments.'

Fortunately, it was a short flight next morning and they were soon driving into the hospital, just after nine o'clock. Miraculously, Jeb had organised a car and driver, was even able to pour hot coffee for her, as they drove from the airfield. A sombre Pete met them as they went into the ward. Jamie was lying pale, immobile and surrounded by machines monitoring her every breath and pulse beat.

'Jamie?' Jacq whispered. 'Jamie, I'm here.'

There was a slight movement but her eyes remained tightly shut.

'She's going to be all right, isn't she?' she asked.

'They think so. She's a very sick girl, though. She has regained consciousness and they say she's just resting now. Best thing for her,' her dad muttered gruffly.

'When did it happen and how exactly?'

'Two days ago.'

'Two days ago? Why didn't you let me know?'

'Didn't know where you were. Jeb's number was recorded on the machine or I wouldn't have been able to call you last night.'

It was a tense few days that followed but they finally began to see some improvement in Jamie. She seemed to have lost none of her mental abilities even though her legs seemed not to belong to her any more. Jeb stayed with them for much of the time, dashing off to conduct his business by phone, until he finally had to leave them.

After a week, Jamie began to undergo more intensive physiotherapy and Jacq and her father spent less time at the hospital and were able to get on with the business of running the farm. They worked from dawn to dusk, pausing only to grab something to eat before dashing to the hospital for their visits.

Jeb phoned regularly, always friendly but largely business like, and never failing to ask after Jamie. Jacq scarcely allowed herself time to think about him, frantically trying to compensate for Jamie's absence on the farm. Finally came the bad news that Jamie's tests had proved largely negative. It seemed unlikely that she would walk again, though a tiny bit of optimism remained, as none of the nerves had been severed. It was a case of waiting to see.

'Jamie, I'm so sorry. It's all my fault. If I hadn't gone off on some hare-brained scheme, you'd never have had to take that group out on your own,' Jacq said disconsolately on her next visit.

'Stop it, Jacq. None of this is your fault. Don't be ridiculous. I need you to be strong for me, not blame yourself and turn into some sort of martyr.'

'I'll look after you, love. I promise.'

' 'Course you will. We'll need some changes in the house though. I'm sorry but I'm going to have to live down-stairs.'

'We've thought of that. We're going to convert the dining-room and put in a shower room for you.'

'But that'll cost a fortune.'

'We'll manage. We can do a lot of work ourselves, and Matt says he'll come and help.'

Jacq was trying desperately to make light of a situation she simply dreaded. They all worked hard enough to keep things afloat and with Jamie a virtual invalid, not only had they lost her contribution but they would always have to spend considerable time helping her with even the simplest tasks. In addition to all of this, Jacq still felt she was partly to blame for leaving Jamie in the first place.

'I suppose I could take over the books and ordering, all that sort of thing. It must help a bit,' Jamie said bravely.

'Don't worry about it, love. We'll manage somehow,' Jacq reassured her.

The next days were a flurry of work in the house, making it ready for Jamie's return. Whatever her sister said, Jacq did feel a sense of being trapped into an indefinite future of working the farm and caring for an invalid.

She took a long ride into the hills the day before Jamie came home, knowing it was probably the last time she would be alone and able to relax this way for many months. She even allowed herself to think of the might-have-been with Jeb. He was still calling her regularly, from Paris, New York, London, Sydney. He certainly covered the globe.

She tried to convince herself that she would have hated the constant travelling, should things have worked out. For a few months, his life sounded like heaven but she knew she would hate that uncertainty for ever. She reigned in her beloved Jasmine and they cantered back down the hills, moving in perfect harmony. With the distant sea shimmering and the lush green of the countryside, she knew this was home — her home.

When she arrived back in the yard, she saw a large car parked to one side. Jeb! Could it really be him? He was the only person with such a car who was likely to visit them. Her heart started pounding and as she led Jasmine into the paddock, her legs felt like jelly. She unsaddled the horse and took the tack into the stable. She kept glancing at the car, her feelings swinging between nerves, annoyance that he should have turned up out of the blue and excitement at the prospect of seeing him again. Maybe it was someone entirely different, she tried to tell herself, but she knew exactly who was visiting.

He was sitting at the worn kitchen table, drinking tea. Her father was chatting easily to him, as if they were old friends, meeting casually to discuss market prices.

'What on earth are you doing here? I thought you were in Australia,' Jacq said sharply, feeling oddly nervous at seeing him again.

'I was, this morning. Though I couldn't be this far south of the equator without dropping by.'

'I don't believe you!' Jacq laughed. 'Oz is miles away. Nowhere near here.'

'I needed to visit New Zealand anyway. Besides, I wanted to see you again. Make sure you really were everything I'd been thinking about.'

Pete rose from his seat, mumbling something about watering plants. Jacq appreciated his tact but felt slightly uncomfortable just the same.

'Jamie's coming home tomorrow,' she said brightly.

'So I understand.'

'One thing. You'll never mistake us again, will you?'

She spoke lightly but the enormity of it all suddenly hit her.

'Oh, Jeb, it's all so awful. I can't imagine how she must feel. Both our lives have been dependent on being able to do everything active. Hobbies, livelihood, everything.'

'I know, love.'

He rose and came to wrap his arms around her.

'It's a terrible thing to have happened, but life goes on and we all have to make the most of it. Now, go and change and we're going to visit Jamie and then I'm taking you out for dinner. No arguments. Your father will be joining us later. We need to finalise the contracts so I thought it might be nice for him to see the hotel for himself.'

'That was a kind thought. I'm sure he'll enjoy the change. He's not really one for eating out. In fact, since Mum died, he's become something of a recluse.'

Jamie was sitting with Matt when they arrived at the hospital. She greeted Jeb with great enthusiasm and thanked him for the huge basket of fruit that was sitting on her bedside locker. Jacq stared. Jeb, it seemed, was even more thoughtful than she'd realised. The four of them chatted comfortably and Jamie kept repeating that she couldn't wait to get home. Pete arrived and the room became a little overcrowded.

'We'll be here first thing to collect you,' Jacq promised. 'See you later, Dad, and 'bye, Matt.'

'I'll be over after work tomorrow evening,' Matt replied. 'If that's OK, of course.'

'Be pleased to see you. Stay for supper. I'll be cooking anyway, so you might as well.'

When they arrived at the Marlow Hotel, Jacq watched as the staff moved forward, almost looking as if they were standing to attention. A clone of the Melissa at the Queenstown hotel smiled and said their table was ready.

'We'll have a drink first. Mr Goodman will be arriving later and we'll eat then.'

'Very good, sir. Where will you be? I'll let you know as soon as he arrives.'

'We'll go to the bar, I think, if that's OK with you, Jacq.'

Jacq nodded and followed him through the imposing doorway. The bar was surprisingly cosy. Small alcoves were sited round the edges and the brightly-lit bar cast pools of light without the room seeming too bright.

'Here's to Jamie,' Jeb toasted when the three of them finally sat down to dinner. 'And to a successful liaison between us all.'

His eyes met Jacq's as he spoke and she read the hidden message, blushing slightly in case her father had also realised what was being said.

'To Jamie,' they repeated.

6

Though delighted to have her twin back home, Jacq often wondered if she had bitten off more than she could chew. There were moments when she felt she could weep with weariness, and the strain of always trying to be cheerful in front of Jamie took its toll. She felt dispirited and her usual fire seemed to have drained right away. But she gritted her teeth and kept going.

Jeb had stayed for a couple of days but had then flown back to England. He continued to phone her and she enjoyed the brief contact with the outside world, certain it wouldn't last much longer. Once he had forgotten about her, and taken up with someone much more suited to his lifestyle, she would never seen him again.

Several times, the thought brought a lump to her throat but she never spoke of it to anyone, especially not Jamie. Her twin felt guilty enough at not being able to pull her weight any more. She herself was having great doubts about Matt's loyalty. He was always with her in the evenings but she felt this was so unfair. She tried to persuade him to go out with other friends, but he stayed by her, always concerned and very loving.

It was another month before Jeb's large car rolled up to the farm once more.

'Why do you never tell us you're coming?' Jacq demanded, caught in a pair of filthy jeans and an old, ripped T-shirt!

'I like to surprise you.' Jeb laughed. 'Besides, I like to see you as you really are, not all tidied up for an occasion.'

'Well, you can certainly see me for the scruff I am. I'll put a kettle on and you can go and talk to Jamie while I take a quick shower. I can't stand the smell of me, even if you don't protest.'

Her heart was doing its usual thudding act the moment she saw him and she fought to resist the temptation to fling her arms round him. After all the days of hard work, he seemed like a breath of fresh air in her rather dull life.

'We're having a roast this evening. Will you stay and eat with us?' she called as she dashed up the stairs.

'Great. Thank you.'

'It has to be the kitchen, I'm afraid. Jamie's taken over the dining-room these days.'

She rushed into the bathroom and began her tidy-up. Her mind was racing through a whole heap of things. Cooking . . . could she manage to spend any time with Jeb . . . and when was she going to fit in Jamie's exercises? Had she finished the orders? Life was just too darned complicated and pleased as she was that Jeb had made time to visit them, she really couldn't spare the time for socialising.

When she came down, Jamie was already in the kitchen, sitting in her wheel-chair.

'Jeb helped me,' she said with a

sunny smile. 'He's much stronger than you. Lifted me with scarcely a murmur.'

'So I should think, great tall bloke like him. Now, Jamie, are you up to peeling a few spuds?'

' 'Course, if you bring them over to me.'

The meal was a great success. Matt came over to join them when he finished his own work for the day and Jeb produced a couple of bottles of good wine and they all relaxed over the well-cooked food. Pete was delighted to have company and took on the rôle of host in a way that the girls hadn't seen for years. Towards the end of the meal, Jeb cleared his throat to speak.

'I have a proposition for Jacq, which you all need to hear as it will affect you all. I've bought a small plane to use when I'm here in New Zealand. It will be used for special guests when they need to move from one place to another, between our hotels and also the new homestead deals we're setting up. I'd like to employ Jacq as pilot, when needed. I'd also like her to spend a couple of weeks flying me around the islands, finalising all our deals.'

'Wow, you'll love that, won't you, Jacq?' Jamie burst out.

'Don't be silly. How can I possibly do anything like that? I'm needed here full time.'

'I'm offering a very generous package. You'll be able to get help for Jamie, the farm, whatever you need. You can even arrange for some specialised treatment for Jamie. In fact, I'll pay for it anyway. I'd be pleased to help in any way I can.'

'Who do you think you are, coming here and flashing your money in front of us? We're not some charity case,' Jacq burst out.

'Jacq,' Pete snapped, 'don't be so rude. You know you'd enjoy the job and it wouldn't be all the time, would it?'

'Certainly not,' Jeb replied. 'A couple of days a week mostly. But I really could do with your help for this initial couple of weeks, and let me help you, too, for Jamie's sake.'

Jamie was sitting pale and anxious in her wheel-chair.

'Do I get a say in all of this?' she asked. 'I think you should do it, Jacq. I am going to get more mobile, even if I can't walk. My arms are gaining strength all the time so I'll soon be able to move myself around much more.'

Jacq said nothing and stared down at her plate. Two whole weeks with Jeb? She just couldn't do it, however much she wanted to. Besides, it would be too dangerous. The others were looking at her, waiting for her response.

'OK. I'll come with you for a few days, but only if we can find someone to come in for Jamie and Dad. It will be expensive though. I'm not just talking anyone. It has to be the right person.'

'There's Mrs Wilbury down the valley. She's a widow and I'm sure she'd be willing. She's strong and an excellent cook,' Matt told them. 'I could have a word with her. She's an old friend of my mum's.'

'We know her. She was also a friend of Mum's,' Jamie added. 'I'm sure she'd be brilliant.'

'Looks like it's all settled then,' Jeb said. 'I'll give you a couple of days to sort things out and then we'll be off. I'll do my best to minimise the time away. Thanks, all of you.'

There was a general murmur and everyone smiled. Jacq suddenly spoke out.

'Why, Jeb? Why are you so intent on disrupting our family like this? What's in it for you?'

Slightly embarrassed, he glanced around the table.

'Shall we talk outside?' he suggested.

'No, let's talk here. I want everyone to hear what you have to say.'

'All right. I think I'm falling in love with you. I know you can't leave your home for long at this particular time, but I'm hoping that if we spend time together, you might forget some of your prejudices. I think we may have the chance of a future together.'

Matt began to clap his hands and went quite pink with pleasure. Pete looked down at his empty cup, clearly uneasy.

'I'll make some more coffee,' he mumbled, as he crossed to the stove.

Jacq was sitting open-mouthed. It was the last thing she had expected to hear and she simply didn't know how to cope with it.

'Well, what do you think?' Jeb asked.

'I think we'd better talk outside. Maybe I shouldn't have insisted that you spoke in front of us all.'

They sat out on the porch, listening to the night sounds. She told him of all her concerns about the differences in their lives. She wasn't a person who could travel endlessly round the world. She needed her base and her family nearby. She didn't dare to tell him, however, that she thought she may be falling in love with him. She needed to keep that information to herself until she could see how the future was going to be. Jamie needed her more than ever now and she wouldn't desert her at this time.

'I'm not even happy at being away for even a few days, not just now.'

'Maybe it was unfair to ask you, but you are a pilot and I genuinely do have to fly all around the place. It's Hal's plane I bought, by the way, so it's one you are used to. I won't try to persuade you. If you think you can do me this favour, I'll be delighted. If you feel your place is here, then so be it. I dare say Hal or someone else will oblige. But it does give me an excuse to offer you a generous amount of money for your services and that must surely help out.'

'You don't have to do that. The going rate would be sufficient. But, OK, I'll come with you for a few days but then we have to say goodbye, for at least the time being anyhow.'

The next day, Jacq whirled around, making endless lists, cooking several dishes to be left in the freezer and trying to pack a few clothes in between.

Finally, Jamie lay back, looking totally exhausted.

'For heaven's sake, Jacq! You're like a whirling dervish. I feel worn out just looking at you. Mrs Wilbury is more than capable of looking after us. Matt will come round in the evenings and Dad is well and truly settled with everything. Now, please sit down and have a cup of herbal tea or something.'

'But there's still a million things to sort out.'

'No, there isn't. Come on. Tell me about Jeb and what you think of him. We haven't had a proper talk in weeks.'

Still protesting and sitting on the edge of her seat, Jacq sipped some tea. Jamie's calm soon reached her and she spoke of her worries about the man with whom she was about to spend the next few days.

'We're just so completely different in every way,' Jacq said unhappily.

'You really do like him though. Love him?'

'Dunno. Even if I do, it's all so

pointless. How long do you think he would be likely to be content with me? Look at me. I'm just a country girl with no sophistication, glamour or anything. He rubs shoulders with gorgeous women all the time, women who spend hours in beauty parlours and health clubs, wear fashionable clothes and eat in posh restaurants all the time. It's never going to work, whatever I might feel about him. I couldn't leave you and Dad for all that.'

By eight the next morning Pete was driving his daughter to the airfield.

'Enjoy yourself, honey,' Pete said. 'You've worked hard the last few weeks. You deserve some time for yourself.'

'Keep in touch though, Dad. Phone me every day and please be honest with me. If you need me to come back, tell me. Don't struggle to manage without me. Promise?'

He nodded his agreement and assured her they'd be just fine. Jeb was waiting by the plane when she arrived and Hal was hovering in the background. He raised a hand to her and she waved back.

'Hal's done a pre-flight check,' Jeb told her.

'I'll still do my own, thanks,' she replied.

No way did she fly a plane without knowing it was all in order, however carefully it had been checked by anyone, even Hal. Jeb smiled and nodded.

⋆ ⋆ ⋆

The trip went well, though it became a bit frantic at times when they had so much to fit in. Occasionally, Jacq met up with old friends at some remote airfields but the pressure of the business gave her little time to relax. Nor did it give her time to brood over the future. What it did prove was that she and Jeb did have a good, easy working relationship and they enjoyed their brief moments together, especially when they were flying. She pointed out places to him and enjoyed the spectacular scenery as they flew over it.

'Maybe one day, we can take time to look at it at ground level,' he shouted through the headphones.

She nodded and smiled back, busy at the controls.

All too soon, they were heading back to Wharenui and all the problems that awaited. So far, Jamie had shown no signs of regaining any movement in her legs and the longer it went on, the less likely it seemed. At least Matt seemed to be standing by her but even that was never totally certain.

'I've enjoyed this week,' Jeb said. 'I hope you have.'

'Of course. Where are we going next?'

'Back to England. I fly out in the morning.'

He kissed her gently before he left, a kiss sweet and tender and full of promise. Jacq felt herself longing for it to go on for ever but she knew now, whatever she might have thought about not fitting into his life, the whole scenario had changed with Jamie's accident. She owed it to her family, her twin in particular, to stay near them.

'Then I guess it's goodbye.'

'I'll keep in touch,' Jeb promised, as he handed her an envelope. 'Your pay.'

He grinned and turned and walked away briskly into the building.

She stuffed the envelope into her bag without looking and followed Jeb to see if her father had arrived to collect her.

When she finally looked at the cheque Jeb had written, she gasped. She had never earned so much money in one go in her life. It was too much, she said, but her father insisted that she banked it, even if she used it to pay for some treatment or help for Jamie.

Her life seemed empty after the excitement of the previous week. She missed Jeb more than she cared to admit. She was half expecting to see his tall frame appearing in the doorway of the little plane; be aware of the scent of his aftershave; listen to his light-hearted chatter when he'd had a successful meeting.

Occasionally, she slipped away for an hour to go riding. She never said much for fear of upsetting Jamie and emphasising things she could no longer do. But it gave Jacq some comfort to be up in the hills and enjoy the feel of her horse and the speed of a gallop as they returned. She was doing her best to push Jeb out of her mind but he was a difficult memory to dislodge.

It took her by surprise one evening when he phoned. He sounded excited and she had to slow him down to understand what he was saying.

'It's an amazing treatment. They've had huge success with it. Being pioneered in the UK. You must bring Jamie over as soon as possible. And don't argue, I'll pay for it. I insist.'

When she finally put down the phone, she looked troubled. It was going to cost a fortune but she knew they had to give Jamie this chance. The family discussed it and all agreed, it certainly merited further investigation.

'Maybe we should accept the payment as a loan from this man of yours,' Pete said unhappily. 'I don't see any other way we're going to raise that sort of money. But we'll pay it back, soon as we can,' he added almost angrily.

'The money he paid me after the flying trip will get us plane tickets. It's a case of when Jamie feels able to make the journey.'

'Maybe in week or two.'

Jamie looked at Matt and reached for his hand.

'I'll help if I can. I have a few savings, though you might have to wait awhile for your ring,' he said, and tears filled Jamie's eyes.

'I didn't think you'd still want us to get engaged. Not now I'm . . . '

'Hush, darling,' Matt said softly. 'You're still you, whatever else happened. And it's you I love. Who knows, if this treatment works, you may well be able to walk again.'

They chatted till late, talking through

the implications of a long trip for the two girls. They all agreed that Jacq must accompany her sister, though it left Pete very short handed. It meant the fruit and vegetable season would not yield the expected profits this year, even with the Marlow contract. Any profit would be swallowed up by taking on extra help.

When Jeb phoned the next evening, Jacq told him their decision and he promised to organise everything.

'You can stay at the hotel while you're over here. I've looked into it and it will take a few weeks of treatment and there may be a further operation needed. Jamie will stay in the clinic and we'll be able to visit her daily.'

'It all sounds wonderful but I could never afford Marlow prices. And before you say it, no, I will not accept a free room.'

'I guessed you'd say that. I shall be taking you on as my personal assistant. You will be arranging all sorts for me and I promise you, I shall work you very hard. It isn't a free trip by any means.'

'Well,' Jacq said thoughtfully, 'OK, as long as I'm earning my keep. Thank you. I'm still not sure why you are being so good to us.'

'Then I'll try to show you when you come over. I've organised air tickets for you. They'll be couriered to you tomorrow and I'll see you in less than a week. Oh, and I'll be meeting you at the airport and don't worry, the airline knows all about Jamie's problems and will make all the arrangements.'

'We leave on Friday,' she then told Jamie. 'I hope you are going to be up to it that soon. Jeb's sending tickets tomorrow.'

She sat down heavily, suddenly half afraid of what had been started.

'He certainly gets things moving, that man of yours,' Pete said.

'He isn't mine,' Jacq protested.

'Oh, no?' Pete said with a grin. 'That's what you think.'

7

It was a long and difficult flight. Though they stayed for a night in Singapore to break the journey, Jamie was in considerable discomfort. Jeb had booked them first-class seats, so at least they had plenty of room and the crew was most helpful, doing whatever they could.

By the time they reached Heathrow, Jamie was pale and exhausted but Jeb had a large limo waiting for them and they were able to relax as they were whisked through the traffic to the hotel. Too weary to talk much, they were grateful when they finally sank into bed that evening.

They both refused dinner, feeling as if they'd done nothing but eat on the flight. Jeb was understanding and took time only to discuss the plans for the following day. Jamie was to go straight to the clinic after breakfast and there, they would assess her and decide on the best course of action.

'Shouldn't she wait a day to recover a little?' Jacq asked.

'The sooner they start, the better. They say it would have been best to begin treatment as soon as possible after the accident so let's not waste any more time.'

Jacq shrugged. If it was OK with Jamie, what was it to her?

Very soon, a routine was established. Each morning, Jacq worked at one side of Jeb's office. She had reasonable skills with the computer so she was able to do what was asked of her. Jeb came and went, spending times at meetings, seeing clients and constantly answering the phone to his father. They usually shared lunch together, sometimes ordering sandwiches and sometimes going out to one of the small restaurants nearby.

At four, they drove to the clinic and spent a couple of hours with Jamie.

She seemed happy enough and with intensive therapy, had even felt the occasional sensation in her legs. She phoned home and spoke to Matt on several occasions and was enjoying British television, reading books from an extensive library and playing music. When Jacq and Jeb left her, they went for dinner at various restaurants and saw a little of the London scene. Jacq was thrilled with it all, though she still missed the outdoors and often felt stifled by the buildings and busy streets. One evening, Jeb asked a favour.

'I know it's a dreadful bore but will you come home with me at the weekend? My father is complaining that he hasn't seen me in ages.'

'Thanks for asking, but I couldn't leave Jamie without a visitor.'

'I'll get one of the girls to go and see her and you can always phone her. I'm sure your sister wouldn't mind for one day. We'd be back Sunday evening, in plenty of time to visit. Please say yes. You could even go out for a ride. My father would be delighted to have your company, I'm sure.'

'I'm not sure I'm ready to go home to meet the parents,' she said lightly.

Finally, she gave in. Jeb always had a habit of getting his own way. They were coming to know each other very well. He kept his promise not to try to push her into anything she didn't want and apart from a gentle good-night kiss, there had been no more physical contact.

Jamie sounded pleased that they were going away for a couple of days and assured Jacq that she would be fine.

They left London after visiting Jamie on the Friday evening. An hour and a half later, they drew up in front of what Jacq could see was a large manor house built of sandy-coloured stone, which glowed to an almost apricot colour in the last of the setting sun. Immaculate grounds surrounded the house and she could see a range of outbuildings stretching to the rear.

'It's beautiful,' Jacq gasped. 'I wish

you'd told me how grand it is. I haven't brought much to wear and certainly nothing posh. I should have gone shopping before we came. Oh, dear, I'm not at all sure about this.'

'You'll be fine,' he told her with a reassuring squeeze of the hand. 'You're beautiful enough without any aids or special clothes. Come on now. Brace yourself to meet the one and only Miles Marlow. Don't worry, you'll twist him round your little finger.'

He led her into the large, imposing hall and pushed the door open to the drawing-room. An older version of Jeb was sitting on a leather sofa, chatting to a beautiful girl, about the same age as Jacq. He stood up and shook hands formally with his son.

'Hello, my boy. Good to see you.'

'And you, Father. I'd like you to meet Jacquetta Goodman. She's over from New Zealand.'

'Pleased to meet you. You enjoying your visit? First time in the UK, is it?'

Shyly she stepped forward and held

out her hand. Miles' large hand covered it and she felt the strength in it. She could see immediately where Jeb was coming from and where his character had been formed. She knew she was going to like this man.

'Yes, it's my first visit to England and I'm enjoying it, despite the circumstances,' she replied.

'Jacq's sister is undergoing some treatment at a London clinic, so things are a bit tense. But, she's making good progress.'

The woman on the sofa coughed, less than discreetly. Jeb's father turned.

'I'm so sorry. This is Lucinda Fletcher. She's been dying to meet you for ages, Jeb. Her father's the director of Fletchers', the sports' car people.'

The leggy blonde unwound herself from the sofa and held out her hand to Jeb. She seemed to draw it close to her, as if trying to absorb him into her aura. Jacq almost laughed at the blatant gesture.

'Jeb Marlow,' she breathed, 'I've been

so looking forward to meeting you. Everyone said you were the catch of the century and I can see why. All this charm as well as looks.'

'Hi,' Jeb stammered, obviously caught unawares. 'Pleased to meet you. May I introduce my fiancée, Jacquetta Goodman?'

'Your what?' Lucinda snapped, her gentle, sexy voice replaced by a much harsher tone.

She turned on Miles.

'I thought you said he was still looking for his ideal woman.'

'I'm as surprised as you are. I had no idea.'

Jacq glared at Jeb, almost speechless. He looked at her with pleading in his eyes. Don't let me down, he was mouthing. Swallowing her angry words, she smiled sweetly.

'I think maybe I won't stay for dinner after all, if you don't mind,' Lucinda simpered to Miles. 'I suddenly remembered I have to be somewhere. Sorry we met just a little too late Jeb, dear. 'Bye.'

She swept out of the room in a cloud of some expensive perfume and shut the door with rather more force than needed.

'I'll go and find Rhea,' Miles said hurriedly. 'She'll want to know you've arrived. Then I'll pour us all a drink before dinner. I suppose it ought to be champagne under the circumstances.'

The moment he shut the door behind him, Jacq turned on Jeb.

'What on earth are you playing at? Fiancée? Me? Did I miss something?'

'Sorry, but you could see how it was. She's about the two hundredth nubile woman he's paraded before me. He's determined to have a flock of grand-children and keeps finding marriageable women, supposedly to tempt me. As if I'd ever settle with some superficial bimbo like that. Anyhow, is it such a dreadful prospect, being married to me?'

'Oh, Jeb, of course not. But just look at all this. Compare it to my home. I'd never have invited you through the door if I'd known your real background.'

'I think it was actually your sister and father who invited me in, if we're making points. But so what? What does where you live matter? It's you I love. I want you, not some farm in the middle of nowhere.'

'I happen to adore that farm,' she said, her voice dangerously low. 'I love living there.'

'I know you do, but you can't intend to stay there for ever, surely?'

She was spared from answering as Miles returned, carrying a tray with an ice bucket, a bottle of the best champagne and four cut glass flutes.

'Here we are. Rhea's just coming. She's sorting the cook out, now that Lucinda has left us. She's rather disappointed, as Lucinda's mother's one of her oldest friends. Still, that's life. Now, Jacquetta, tell me all about yourself. How long have you and Jeb known each other and what is more, why didn't I know anything about this engagement till now?'

'It was all a bit sudden,' Jeb replied.

'You can say that again,' Jacq agreed. 'Very sudden.'

'You're not wearing a ring.'

'No. We haven't had time to get one yet.'

'Just as well.' Miles grinned. 'There's a piece of family jewellery just waiting for this occasion. Belonged to my mother. I'll get it right away.'

Jacq's cheeks burned. This was getting worse by the moment.

'I couldn't. I mean, it's very good of you but . . . '

'I won't hear a word of it. Of course you must have it. Rhea doesn't like emeralds and she never wanted it. Do you have any objections to emeralds?'

'Well, no, of course not.'

He nodded and, smiling again, went out of the room to his study.

'You've got to do something,' Jacq hissed. 'I can't accept a family heirloom! For heaven's sake! What have you done?'

'Rather well, I think.'

The door opened and Rhea, Jeb's stepmother, came into the room. She was considerably younger than her husband and what Jacq considered a typical trophy wife. She shook hands with Jacq, briefly touching Jeb's arm in recognition of his arrival. There was no warmth in her eyes as she looked Jacq up and down. Obviously, the girl was not dressed as smartly as she should have been and the look of disdain was not lost on her.

'Perhaps you should show her up to her room, Jeb. I expect she'd prefer to change for dinner.'

'I don't think so,' Jeb replied. 'We've had a long day. We'll probably go to bed early and wake up early tomorrow.'

'As you like. I was thinking of Jac . . . what did you say the name was? Something ethnic, from New Zealand, I suppose, wasn't it?'

Jacq refused to be baited and, uncharacteristically, remained silent. Jeb's mouth twitched as he saw her mammoth efforts not to complicate matters further. Miles returned with a small, leather ring box and handed it to Jeb. He suggested that they might prefer to look at it later and thus avoid embarrassment if Jacq didn't like the ring. She felt it was very thoughtful of him and decided that she really liked Jeb's father. She relaxed for the rest of the evening and even coped with a congratulatory toast in champagne.

When they finally escaped upstairs, Jeb took out the box and opened it. He held it out to her. She gazed at the exquisite jewel. It was a huge emerald, surrounded by tiny diamonds, set on a simple gold band.

'Oh, it's gorgeous,' she breathed. 'Must be worth a fortune.'

'Try it,' Jeb ordered.

He held it out to her and slipped it on her finger. It could have been made just for her. He drew her towards him and put his arms round her.

'I love you, Jacq,' he whispered.

'Oh, Jeb, it's lovely but it isn't mine. Never will be.'

'It could be.'

He covered her mouth with his and she felt herself drawn close to him. She was lost in the tenderness of his kiss, the sheer sweetness of the taste of him. She knew secretly that she had surrendered.

'Stop it, Jeb. You are taking unfair advantage of me. I won't be coerced in this way. Keep your ring. I can't marry you.'

'Please. At least pretend, just for this weekend. You can see how pleased my father is.'

'But Rhea isn't. She hates me. I can tell.'

'She doesn't. She's simply disappointed that I haven't taken up her candidate.'

'Candidate? You make it sound like an election. All the same, she doesn't approve of me. She thinks I'm a frump from the sticks, which I am. And this talk of a special party to celebrate tomorrow evening. I don't have anything to wear to a do like that.'

'We'll go and buy you something. Oxford's only a short drive. We'll get you something exotic, to go with an emerald engagement ring. Do this for me and I promise I won't keep you to it later. You owe me this at least.'

Of course she owed him. She owed him big time. How could she refuse? If he wanted to dress her up in some stupid posh frock, she'd go along with it, for Jamie's sake. It was all for Jamie's sake. Jacq Goodman never wore posh frocks and knew nothing of mixing with people in some big country club. She wasn't even sure she knew which knife and fork to use if there were more than one! In fact, she felt quite sick at the whole thought of a big party where she might be on show.

She swayed slightly on her feet, suddenly overcome with the enormity of what was happening. She should have stayed at home, and settled for dependable, solid Hal. Jeb's arms came out to steady her and he held her tight. She looked up at him. His eyes were closed. He sensed her gaze and opened them again, looking down into her deep brown eyes.

'I wish you could feel for me, as I feel for you. I do love you, Jacq.'

'Oh, Jeb,' she whispered, not daring to admit her own feelings. 'I'll see you in the morning.'

At breakfast the next morning, Miles was out somewhere and Rhea made it quite clear that she disapproved of Jacq. She was disdainful about her clothes, her hairstyle and even suggested her own manicurist might possibly squeeze her in during the morning. One could hardly display a family heirloom on work hands, could one? Jacq made no comment, biting back her fury so that she didn't upset either Jeb or his father.

'We're going into Oxford first thing. Jacq didn't expect celebrations this weekend so she didn't bring anything appropriate to wear,' Jeb said icily.

'I expect you'd like my advice, wouldn't you? I could just about fit in a trip to Oxford between hair and nails.

In fact, why don't just the two of us go and then we can get you a make-over at the same time. I'm sure you won't want to let Jeb down in front of all his friends and business colleagues.'

'Jeb and I will go together, thanks all the same. He doesn't think I'll let him down, even if I do look like a country bumpkin. After all, we are still in the country, aren't we?'

Rhea glared.

'We have standards, even in the country,' she snapped. 'Please yourself. I was only trying to help. We obviously come from different worlds, dear.'

'Excuse me,' Jacq said, dumping her napkin in the middle of her unfinished meal. 'I've lost my appetite.'

She stormed out of the room and went outside. It was drizzling with rain but she didn't care. How could Jeb put her through this? She went to the back of the house and wandered into what was obviously a stable yard. A tall chestnut stallion peered over the stable door and she walked over to pet him.

He nuzzled her hand and she patted him, talking softly to him.

'You're a beauty, aren't you?'

'He certainly is. My favourite. I take it you ride.'

Miles spoke with enthusiasm when near his horses. Jacq swung round.

'Sorry, I didn't realise you were there. I think I miss my horses more than anything at the moment. Mind you, none of them comes near this sort of quality, but they are all so beautiful.'

'Would you like to go for a ride with me? I'm about to get Prince saddled. You could try Blossom there, if you think you can manage her and don't mind a bit of English drizzle.'

'I'd love it. Thanks. Oh, but I'm supposed to be going out to buy something to wear for this party thing tonight.'

'And which would you rather do?'

'No question, but Rhea seems to think I should be spending the day getting myself made-over or something. And I really do have nothing with me that's suitable for tonight.'

'Jeb can take you this afternoon. Let's tell him you're coming for a ride and then you can go shopping this afternoon. As for one of Rhea's make-overs, I think you look perfectly fine as you are. Don't deprive me of this chance to get to know my future daughter-in-law.'

Half an hour later, Miles and Jacq rode off through the extensive parkland surrounding the house. Jeb had been amused at the change of plan and Rhea had driven off in a huff, presumably to her beauty treatment.

'I'm afraid your wife doesn't approve of me,' Jacq said as they trotted along among the trees.

'Take no notice of her. She's quite harmless really and she's put out that Lucinda isn't going to be joining the family.'

'But Lucinda would really be so much more suitable than I am. I don't belong among all this.'

She waved her hand at the

beautifully-tended fields, all looking as if they'd been cut like lawns.

'Do you love my boy?' Miles asked suddenly.

'Yes,' she admitted. 'I believe I do. But I'm still afraid it's doomed to failure. We're total opposites, Jeb and I. My dad farms vegetables and kiwi fruit. We live in a ranch-style house, nothing fancy. We all work hard and if it wasn't for my sister's accident and this treatment, I'd never have left.'

'I like you. I gather you knew nothing of this so-called engagement, probably not before you arrived here, did you?'

'No,' Jacq admitted. 'How did you know?'

'I suspect it was Jeb's ploy to be rid of the lovely Lucinda. Oh, don't worry. It's happened before. You happened to be conveniently on hand.'

He laughed a warm, friendly chuckle.

'All the same, I can see why my son's so smitten. Never seen him this committed before. Now, let's put you through your paces.'

He nudged his horse and he immediately broke into a trot. Jacq did the same and soon they were galloping free, nothing in their way for a couple of miles. She kept up with the slightly larger horse and finally they reined in, breathless and laughing.

'That was terrific,' Jacq said happily. 'Felt so good. Your Blossom is glorious. Such a powerful creature. Thank you so much.'

'You look better, too, less strained. The worry lines are fading. But, all good things come to an end. We'd better get back, have a spot of lunch and then you can go and buy something glitzy for tonight. Sorry to inflict it on you but Rhea wanted to make a splash and it's a good way of announcing to the county that Jeb's no longer available. Whatever happens long term, we must go through with it for now. Who knows? You may come to like the idea when you're used to it. We usually get a stream of hopefuls whenever he's at home. I suspect it's the family fortune that helps, but he's not a bad chap, I guess. You know, I'm pleased you have doubts about your differences. It's a healthy sign. Now, first back pays for champagne tonight.'

Jacq laughed. It was out of her character to throw a race but this time, she might just let him win.

'I like your girl,' Miles told Jeb later. 'She's made of the right stuff. Congratulations, my boy. You made a good choice. I . . . er . . . no. It's all right.'

'What? Well, thanks, Dad. I thought once you'd seen her ride that you might approve. She's good, isn't she? But maybe there's something you should know.'

Jeb was feeling bad about what had started as a small deception.

'Tell me later. I need a shower and then we'll have some lunch. Rhea still out?'

Jeb nodded, knowing the moment for confession had passed. He went to find Jacq and found her on the phone to

Jamie. She covered the mouthpiece and turned to him.

'She's fine. Just wanted to touch base. Look, Jamie, I'll have to go now. Speak later. Love you. Yes, that's fine. 'Bye.'

She put down the phone and turned to Jeb.

'Sorry, I'm keeping you waiting. I like your father, by the way. He's a good man.'

'The feeling's mutual. He thinks I made a good choice. It's OK. I know we made a deal.'

Jacq smiled to herself. She was not going to let Jeb know about his father's discussion with her.

Jacq enjoyed the party much more than she would have believed possible. The simple green silk dress that had cost more than her normal annual clothes budget fitted her perfectly and the precious ring was a perfect match. She even felt glamorous for the first time in her life and having the most handsome man in the room dancing attendance on her made her feel very special. When they finally arrived back home, the party was deemed a great success. Rhea, too, seemed to have enjoyed herself, despite the earlier negativity.

'I'll go and organise some coffee,' she announced and left them.

Jeb noticed the answering machine light flashing and pressed the replay button. It was Jamie and alarm bells at once flashed in Jacq's mind. She dashed over to the machine and listened to her sister's message. She sounded tearful and anxious.

'Can you phone Dad, as soon as you get this message? There's a problem at home. Sorry to interrupt your weekend, Jacq, but it sounds very urgent. He wouldn't tell me what was wrong.'

'It's too late to phone Jamie. She must be asleep by now,' Jacq said anxiously. 'Do you mind if I phone New Zealand? It'll be about midday there.'

'Of course you must phone,' Miles

told her. 'I'll go and keep Rhea out of the way.'

With trembling fingers, Jacq dialled her home number. The phone rang for ages and she was about to give up when she heard her father's voice.

'Dad? I just got Jamie's message. Whatever's happened?'

She listened for a few moments, her face paling as she heard the news. Jeb was practically bouncing up and down to hear what was being said.

'I'll catch the first flight possible. I'll sort something out. I expect Jeb will visit Jamie. She'll understand. Now don't worry more than you can help. We'll get through this, Dad, I'm sure. 'Bye and I love you.'

Briefly, she told Jeb the dreadful news. One of their workers in the kiwi fields had died in an accident. They claimed he was suffering from side effects after the spraying of the fruit with a certain chemical.

'I can't believe Dad would ever let anyone work with that stuff unless they were fully protected. The chap turned the tractor over and was crushed. The family claims he was high on the chemical spray and that my father's liable for compensation. The insurance probably wouldn't pay up if he was negligent. Dad says it's the end of everything. If their claim is successful, he'll have to sell up and . . . '

She burst into tears.

'How could I have been enjoying myself at a stupid, pointless party when all this was going on? And what was I thinking about, leaving Jamie with all this?'

'Now calm down. Stop blaming yourself for everything that goes wrong.'

'It's my punishment for thinking I could possibly have any sort of future with you. Ever since we met everything's gone wrong.'

'Don't be ridiculous. Now, let's get down to the practicalities. I'll get on to the airlines and book us on the first flight tomorrow.'

'Us? You ought to stay and be with Jamie.'

'Nonsense. Matt can come over and be with her. Do you know his number?'

Within the hour, Jeb had organised everything. Jacq was staggered at the speed with which it all happened. They spoke to Matt and he agreed immediately. Reinforced with coffee, Jeb and Jacq drove back to London and flung a few clothes into a bag and were soon driving to Heathrow, as dawn was breaking. Exhausted, they both slept for much of the flight and soon, they were in Singapore, waiting for the onward connection.

'We might even bump into Matt. He's due here any time.'

'Now that would be just too much.' Jacq managed to smile. 'You realise I didn't even call Jamie before we left, it was all such a rush.'

He handed her his mobile.

'I don't know the number.'

He took it from her and scrolled down the list. He pressed a button and handed it back. She quickly told Jamie the latest developments and wept with her sister at the generosity of Jeb's actions, especially flying Matt over to look after her.

'He's a very special man,' she said, looking down at her engagement finger, where the family ring was still in place. 'Would you believe we got engaged last night?'

Jeb stared at her, his face breaking into a broad grin.

'You actually admitted it to your sister,' he said incredulously.

The whoop of delight from the other end of the phone told him that Jacq's sister approved of the match. The next few minutes were spent in delighted exchanges.

'Hey, there's Matt,' Jeb called out. 'Over here. Come and speak to Jamie.'

It all seemed so unbelievable that Jacq had to keep pinching herself to believe it was true. She'd been on an emotional roller coaster for weeks, it seemed. Somehow, agreeing to be engaged to Jeb had happened amidst too many other things and it was almost easier to go with it than keep fighting it. They tried to catch up on the news as quickly as possible, knowing time was limited.

'I have to go,' Matt announced. 'See you soon and, Jeb, I can't thank you enough for organising all this.'

'Organising's what I do,' he said calmly. 'Give our love to Jamie and wish her luck. Speak soon. Safe flight.'

The final drive up to the farm was almost the longest part of the trip. Jacq was impatient, wishing the hire car could go faster. Her father greeted her with a desperate hug. Jeb watched them and realised how close this family was compared to his own. His family never said they loved each other; they never hugged or even touched each other except for a formal shake of the hands. Jacq was right. There were great gulfs between them but he felt confident that they would overcome them. He stood back, feeling isolated from the girl he

161

loved and her father.

Once the greetings were over and Jamie's progress was discussed, they began to take stock of the situation here. The Press had got the story and the phone had been ringing so much that Pete had finally taken it off the hook. Together, they worked out a plan of action, in which Jeb figured highly. He gave Pete his own mobile phone, for emergencies and so they could keep in touch. He would pick up another when he got to the hotel.

He was going to consult with their own company lawyers to see what could be done. Meanwhile he advised them to continue to keep silent regarding the Press. After a quick meal, he left them and drove back down to the town.

The next couple of days were like some sort of nightmare. Every time Jacq or Pete showed their faces through the door, someone rushed forward with a camera. The farm work had to be left and she could scarcely even get out to feed the horses. Fortunately, the spring pasture was rich and she merely needed to check on the water and see they were all in good condition. It was hard to believe that less than a week ago, she was riding through a lush country park in the Oxfordshire autumn.

Jeb had called a couple of times but seemed to have made himself busy with other matters, she assumed. Odd people came and went outside the house but she largely ignored them. Pete became more and more despondent as the unaccustomed days of waiting went on.

'I think I'm almost ready to give in,' he said wearily as they sat down to supper one evening. 'It just isn't worth the effort any more. You and Jamie will be leaving anyway before long. What point is there, trying to keep this place going? I'll settle for the best offer and be done with it. Not that anyone's going to offer much under the circumstances.'

'Oh, Dad, you can't give in.'

'But all this Press nonsense. We're

like prisoners in our own house. I'll never recover from this bad publicity. They're saying that I don't care, and mud sticks. What's that going to do to my business?'

Jacq left the table and went to the door. It was almost dark but still the group of reporters was standing outside the house. As the door opened, flash bulbs went off and a cameraman raised a large recording machine to his shoulders.

'Miss Goodman, have you any comment to make? Do you admit negligence?'

'I don't understand why you think you can persecute us this way. We've done nothing wrong, and we admit to nothing. Now, please let us get on with our lives.'

'So you don't take any responsibility for the family's loss? Will Browning was only thirty years old. He had three children, all under ten. Don't you feel you owe them something?'

'I'm making no comment. It's in the

hands of a solicitor. Now clear off.'

She went back inside, shaking with anger.

'They won't leave, you know,' Pete said.

'I don't care. I'm sick of them. Tomorrow I'm going out riding. If they all want to come with me, more fools them. I refuse to let our lives be ruined by the media circus. It's not as if we did anything wrong. You told the wretched man to wear protective gear.'

Her father nodded but looked positively grey with worry.

There was a call from Jeb early next morning. He asked if they'd seen the papers, which of course they hadn't.

'Oh, Jacq, why did you have to speak to them? They've really gone to town. **Farmers Show No Sympathy** is the kindest of the headlines. I won't even read the rest to you. I'll be coming up later today. We'll discuss what to do next when I see you.'

She frowned and went out to saddle up Jasmine. Whatever they said or did, she was going to show them that she wasn't going to be browbeaten this way. There was a chorus of questions as she walked over to the paddock and the flash bulbs were going off non-stop. She whistled her horse and she came trotting over immediately. Ignoring everyone, she fastened the saddle and mounted the horse, riding through the middle of the group. As soon as she could, she trotted the horse up the steep paths, the journalists struggling to follow her.

She made a great play of inspecting the kiwi vines, peering down from the saddle to look at the state of the ripening fruit. In and out of the rows she went, hopefully giving the journalists some much-needed exercise. Once she had covered the first field, sheltered by the high hedges, she went through the gap and into the next field. The journalists began to fall back, realising what she was doing and they waited at the end of the rows.

If they printed pictures of her

apparently out riding without a care in the world, she could argue that she needed to inspect their crops.

When her inspection was complete, she rode back to the house, leaving Jasmine in the paddock and still saying nothing to the waiting knot of people.

Jeb arrived just as she got back and he stormed past the throng, ignoring them. He greeted Jacq with a kiss.

'Our legal chap is coming up soon to make a statement. It's good news.'

'What's going on?' Pete asked.

'Your worker, Will Browning, is a well-known drunk apparently. He'd been out celebrating with his mates the night before the accident. He was nowhere near the chemical and certainly this was not the cause of the accident. According to one of the barmen, he had at least ten pints of lager that night and that was only in the one bar. Given the fact that he had a heart condition and was also on medication, he would probably have killed himself anyway. He was in no condition to be driving anything, let alone a tractor. You certainly couldn't be expected to conduct a daily medical examination on your employees.'

'Heart condition? He swore to me that he was in good health before I signed him on. In fact, I must have his contract somewhere. He signed the declaration himself.'

'That's brilliant,' Jacq told Jeb. 'But how did you find out?'

'I hired a private detective, of course. Now, are you going to offer me some coffee or do I have to make it myself?'

'I don't know how we shall ever repay you, for this and everything else,' Pete said gruffly. 'My family will be indebted to you for ever.'

'Nonsense. What's the point of having money if you can't use it to do some good? Besides, I'm hoping that you will be my family very soon, assuming Jacq hasn't changed her mind?'

He reached for her hand and looked for his ring.

'I've put it away safely,' she said. 'Hardly the sort of thing one wears around here. But I don't want to marry you because we are indebted to you. Besides, you've seen what happens if ever I go away from here.'

'I've been thinking about all that. If it's the travelling you don't like, I'll resign from my job. We can buy something near here and I'll come to live in New Zealand with you.'

'You'd do that for me?'

''Course. I couldn't bear to live without you, Jacq. And I'm also authorised to make you an offer for the farm, Pete. My father likes the idea of the company owning the farm that supplies our produce. The condition is, of course, that you continue to act as manager. You'd have full control, just as you do now and a decent salary to go with it.'

The rest of the day passed in a frenzy of Press statements, TV interviews and long talks about the future. When darkness fell, Jeb and Jacq stood outside the house, looking over the valley that was her beloved home.

'You do love me, don't you?' Jeb whispered.

''Course I do.'

'And you no longer worry about our lives being too different?'

'Well,' she murmured. 'Maybe not so different, given a few changes.'

8

After a couple of days, things were more or less back to normal on the farm. Pete set out early to work, vowing he'd never complain again about having too much to do. The days of enforced idleness when he thought he was about to lose everything had certainly taught him a lesson. He was considering Jeb's offer and had almost made up his mind to sell and be rid of the responsibility.

Jeb was in town, working as usual and Jacq was doing her own chores around the house, when she heard a vehicle approaching and went to look out. She was half expecting Jeb and assumed he'd freed himself a bit earlier than he'd thought.

It was a huge car stopping, she realised, and ran casual fingers through the hair that was escaping from its pony tail. To her utter amazement, she saw

Miles Marlow climbing out of the rear, together with Jeb.

'Goodness, what ever are you doing here?' she asked as she joined them, still in shock.

'Hello, my dear. I thought it was time I came to visit. See what it is about this place that makes my son want to give up his excellent job.'

'Come in. You'll have to excuse the mess. I was having a bit of a turnout. We've been somewhat stressed of late and nothing's been done. Would you like some coffee?'

'Love some. Is your father around? I'd like to meet him.'

'I'll ring the bell. He should be able to hear it OK.'

She clanged the huge, old bell they used to call each other back for meals, then went inside, followed by Jeb and his father. She put the coffee pot on the stove and offered Miles a chair.

'I'm afraid things are somewhat cramped since Jamie's accident. We turned the dining-room into a bedroom for her and everywhere else seems to have been condensed into this room.'

'Relax, Jacq. I'm not here to inspect you or where you come from. I'm quite satisfied that you are good folk and you're not out to get your claws into my son's money. Now, do I get a kiss from my son's fiancée?'

Jeb stared at his father. He was unaccustomed to any display of affection and watched as Jacq went to him shyly and kissed his cheek. She glanced at Jeb and smiled at him.

'I'm glad we passed,' she said with a grin.

'I'm afraid I did a bit of checking. Can't be too careful, especially after all that unpleasant nonsense with your worker.'

'You did what? You checked us out? How dare you?' she snapped, suddenly dismayed and turned away from him, fuming.

'I'm sorry, but I couldn't allow the Marlow name associated with any scandal.'

'It was Father who organised the private detective to find out about your worker. He naturally had to find out all he could about your business at the same time,' Jeb interrupted.

'I'm not happy about you spying on us. What would he have done if he'd discovered we weren't completely honest? Tried to split us up? Refuse to allow us to marry?'

'He wouldn't have succeeded. I've told you, I'll give up my job and any association with Marlow Hotels, if that's what it takes.'

'I've reached a decision. I'm going to retire completely,' Miles put in. 'You can have the family house in Oxfordshire. It's the right time. My wedding gift to you both. I want a smaller place, somewhere warm. Probably the Mediterranean or somewhere. Might even consider a place in Auckland. We could split our time between the two.'

'What does Rhea think of all this?' Jeb asked totally take aback by the announcement.

'Haven't told her. Worked it all out on the flight.'

'So, Jeb would be in charge of everything?' Jacq asked.

'Indeed. I think he's ready now he's finally settling down. He can employ someone to do the legwork and settle down, pretty much as I did. Give you plenty of time and opportunity to produce me a few grandchildren.'

'Sorry, Father, but I told you, I just resigned,' Jeb said firmly.

Jacq stepped forward and put her arm through Jeb's.

'I don't know why you think I'm worth all this, but I can't let you give up something that is in your blood.'

Jacq smiled at the man she loved more than anything.

'I'm sure we can come to some arrangement about where we live, as long as I can spend plenty of time here.'

The rest of the day was spent showing Miles around the farm. He admired the horses and said all the right things about the way things were managed. He and Pete got on surprisingly well and talked for long periods while Jeb and Jacq were busy making their own plans.

'I want to be married from here,' Jacq insisted. 'But I can't do it until Jamie is better. Even in a wheel-chair, she has to be bridesmaid. I hope you understand. And I want a simple, country wedding. No frills and exotic trimmings.'

'Whatever you want, my love. We'll have a job explaining it all to Rhea but she's not the important one. There'll be loads of people disappointed that we're not being married in England.'

'Too bad,' Jacq said firmly.

★   ★   ★

Two months later, Jamie flew home. She was much stronger and able to stand a little and almost able to walk again. It would take many more months of hard work and physiotherapy but she had got movement and sensation back in her legs.

She flung herself into the wedding plans and helped choose their dresses. Jacq insisted it would be a simple dress and refused to accept any of Jeb's offers of money. They did, however, compromise when it came to the reception and agreed that it should be held in the Marlow Hotel, in town. As she said, it would look bad if they didn't and Miles would never have forgiven them if he wasn't allowed some contribution.

The weather on the wedding day was perfect. Jamie and Matt set off early for the church to give them time to get settled with the wheel-chair before too many of the guests had arrived. It was quite an affair for the little town and everyone seemed to have turned out to see the local girl and the famous family joined together. At the farm, Jacq came down the stairs to her father and he took her arm, pulling her to him.

'You look wonderful, my darling girl. I'm so proud of you. Are you ready? Let's go.'

They drove down the long track and

down the hill to the town.

'Goodness, look at all these people. I feel like royalty.'

She waved as they passed and smiled happily at everyone. When they arrived at the church, she saw Jamie still outside.

'Why isn't she inside, waiting?' Jacq muttered. 'I hope she's all right.'

Jacq got out of the car with scant regard for her long white dress and rushed over to her sister.

'What is it, Jamie? Are you OK? Why aren't you waiting inside as we arranged?'

'Because I've got a surprise for you. As long as you don't mind Matt joining the procession, I'm going to walk down the aisle with you. I was never going to let you do it alone.'

Jacq's eyes filled with tears and she held on to her father, shaking as she walked into the little church. She saw Jeb waiting at the altar, surrounded by a vast array of friends from all over. But all the time, she was watching her sister as she bravely walked the long distance down the aisle, holding on to Matt. Jeb was openly moved at the sight and she saw tears in his eyes when she arrived at his side.

'Thank you, Jamie,' she whispered. 'That was the best wedding present I could have had.'

Then she turned back to her groom.

After the ceremony and reception were over, Jeb handed her a package.

'This is my wedding gift to you, though you may not want to keep it.'

Intrigued, she opened it and looked inside. It was the deeds to the farm.

'It's yours. You can give it to your father if you want to.'

'Oh, Jeb, why are you so good to us?'

'Because I love you. Now come here, Mrs Marlow. We need some time together before we start organising another wedding.'

'Jamie and Matt, I know. They are following us down the aisle as soon as we can arrange it. Isn't life wonderful?'

'It certainly is,' he agreed, and sealed it with a kiss.

We do hope that you have enjoyed
reading this large print book.

Did you know that all of our titles
are available for purchase?

We publish a wide range of high
quality large print books including:
**Romances, Mysteries, Classics
General Fiction
Non Fiction and Westerns**

Special interest titles available in
large print are:
**The Little Oxford Dictionary
Music Book, Song Book
Hymn Book, Service Book**

Also available from us courtesy of
Oxford University Press:
**Young Readers' Dictionary
(large print edition)
Young Readers' Thesaurus
(large print edition)**

For further information or a free
brochure, please contact us at:
**Ulverscroft Large Print Books Ltd.,
The Green, Bradgate Road, Anstey,
Leicester, LE7 7FU, England.
Tel:** (00 44) **0116 236 4325
Fax:** (00 44) **0116 234 0205**

Other titles in the
Linford Romance Library:

AN AUSTRIAN AFFAIR

Sheila Benton

Lisa is a driver for her family firm, which runs coach tours abroad. On a trip to Austria, she meets Mark Treherne, who constantly asks questions about the company. She senses Mark is no ordinary tourist and feels he is reporting on her organisation. Later, when her father telephones to say they have been taken over by Treherne Holdings, Lisa bitterly confronts Mark. However, she has to apologise to him when she discovers her father's job is secure . . .

SO GOLDEN THEIR HARVEST

Jane Carrick

Susan and Hazel had looked after their father since their mother's death, but now Susan is to marry Colin, a farmer, and move to Australia. However, after Colin's Gran has a fall, the old lady begs him to take over her run-down farm in Scotland instead. Susan doesn't mind and works hard with Colin to build up the farm. Peter, one of the farm hands, falls in love with Susan, but she has eyes only for Colin. When Hazel visits Susan, she finds herself attracted to the handsome Peter, but he tells her of his love for her sister.

DARK SHADDOWS

Joyce Johnson

When heiress Sophie Rivers accidentally discovers Richard Weatherby was marrying her to retrieve him from bankruptcy, she flees the wedding ceremony and assumes a new identity in rural Barton. Here Sophie discovers unexpected talents in a craft community, and she meets Ben Fairfield, who helps her come to terms with her unhappiness. Sophie's true identity is discovered when Richard finds her, but she also learns Ben has his own guilty secret to conceal.

IN SUNSHINE AND IN SHADOW

Ravey Sillars

For Nicola, her summer vacation job — looking after an adorable little boy named Carlo — is a dream come true. But with the growing fear of kidnap, the dream is becoming a nightmare. Both Carlo's grandfather and his father, Angelo (who is working undercover for the Carabinieri) are widowers. Amidst the summer crowds on the Amalfi Coast, it is Nicola's job to keep their beloved child safe. She will do it if it kills her. But she must on no account fall in love with the disturbingly attractive Angelo.

SWEET SONG OF LOVE

Mavis Thomas

When her sister Sarah's marriage breaks up, Meriel Maynard abandons her happy London life and takes Sarah and her young daughter, Jasmine, to help out at their aunt's country guest house, hoping Sarah will benefit from a change of scene. Meriel soon becomes interested in a local Academy of Art and Music — and in its Director, the difficult and strangely attractive Rex Hazelwood. She somehow finds herself heavily embroiled in Rex's campaign to save the failing Academy, and in his disturbing family conflicts . . .

TO FORGET THE PAST

Pia Walton

Tessa Robson is stunned to meet a man she hoped never to see again, but living in a nearby cottage on the estate, meeting Josh Maitland is unavoidable. When Tessa learns of his wife's death and that he is the father of a little boy, she relents, becomes a friend and then loves Josh and James. However, whilst shopping in Newcastle, she is incensed to see Josh kissing a redheaded female, and when she returns home she discovers James is missing . . .